James Fawckner Nicholls

The Remarkable Life, Adventures and Discoveries of Sebastian

Cabot

James Fawckner Nicholls

The Remarkable Life, Adventures and Discoveries of Sebastian Cabot

ISBN/EAN: 9783337341817

Printed in Europe, USA, Canada, Australia, Japan

Cover: Foto ©Andreas Hilbeck / pixelio.de

More available books at **www.hansebooks.com**

THE REMARKABLE LIFE, ADVENTURES

AND DISCÓVERIES

OF

SEBASTIAN CABOT,

OF BRISTOL,

THE FOUNDER OF GREAT BRITAIN'S MARITIME POWER,

DISCOVERER OF AMERICA, AND ITS

FIRST COLONIZER.

BY J. F. NICHOLLS,

CITY LIBRARIAN, BRISTOL.

LONDON:

SAMPSON LOW, SON, AND MARSTON,

CROWN BUILDINGS, FLEET STREET.

1869.

CHISWICK PRESS:—PRINTED BY WHITTINGHAM AND WILKINS,
TOOKS COURT, CHANCERY LANE.

TO

THE RIGHT WORSHIPFUL

FRANCIS ADAMS, Esquire,

THE MAYOR,

THE WORSHIPFUL THE ALDERMEN, THE HIGH SHERIFF,

THE MEMBERS OF THE TOWN COUNCIL, AND

J. F. LUCAS, Esquire,

THE MASTER,

THE WARDENS, AND COMMONALTY, OF THE SOCIETY

OF MERCHANT ADVENTURERS OF THE

CITY OF BRISTOL,

𝕿𝖍𝖎𝖘 𝕸𝖔𝖓𝖔𝖌𝖗𝖆𝖕𝖍 of

SEBASTIAN CABOT,

A FELLOW CITIZEN,

IS RESPECTFULLY DEDICATED.

PREFACE.

HAKLUYT, a Prebendary of Briftol, in 1584, in writing the "Early
Hiftory of Maritime Enterprife,"
conferred a great boon on all fuc-
ceeding hiftorians; but it muft be allowed that,
occafionally, he took great liberties with the
text of his authorities.

His errors have been followed to a greater
or leffer extent, by our principal naval writers,
who were moft of them content to accept his
authority without the trouble of further fearch.

Thus the three or more voyages of Cabot
are jumbled together in Ramufio's ftatement
altered by Hakluyt, and again by his copyifts,
leaving the whole a contradictory and bewilder-
ing puzzle to all who read the differing ftatements.

The writer has felt that the recent difcovery
in the "Bibliothèque Imperial" of a map of

Cabot, dated 1544, gives a key to the enigma, and the following pages attempt to define the feparate voyages, the object and refults of each, from a careful analyfis of all the evidence at command.

Still, had Biddle's memoir of Sebaftian Cabot (A.D. 1831) been written in a concifer and clearer ftyle, with lefs of petulance and hypercriticifm, the probabilities are that this attempt would never have been made.

His work is full of hiftoric refearch, and has done good fervice; the writer has drawn largely from his materials, and defires to acknowledge the obligation.

Differing widely from him on fome points, it is but right to add that the author's conclufions have been mainly arrived at through evidence which was not known to be in exiftence thirty years fince.

This additional evidence created a defire to clear the character of a fellow-citizen, and to place him in his proper pofition before the world.

For that Cabot was really a great man, few or none who read thefe pages will difpute.

Nor does his greatnefs arife from the mere accident of difcovery. What he found he fought for, or, at all events, its equivalent; whilft his whole life manifefts a perfiftent, energetic determination to attain a given ob- ject; combined with a capacious power of in- tellect, which enabled him to grafp, determine, explain, and apply problems in fcience that his contemporaries underftood not.

In him was the proverb verified: "Seeft thou a man diligent in bufinefs? he fhall ftand before kings; he fhall not ftand before mean men." The haughty grandees of Spain owned him as their peer, whilft the nobleft blood of England held office under him.

The man who could not only come out un- fcathed from the hotbed of tyranny, licentious cruelty, and debafing fuperftition which Spain and the Spanifh poffeffions in America openly difplayed in that age, but could pen thofe prudent, wife, and pious inftructions which he gave to the men whom he felected and em- ployed, muft ever be entitled to the epithet of a great man.

What he did for his country, its commerce

and its fhipping, the following pages will in fome meafure indicate.

Though his duft lies in an unknown and unhonoured grave, and his ftatue graces neither palace nor city, if this work fhould clear for him a niche in the memory of his countrymen, it will be by them fpeedily filled, for

"A good man's deeds are his beft monument;"

And Sebaftian Cabot will henceforth have a home in every Englifh heart, as well as in that of the great nation who dwell in the land which he firft difcovered, and which ought at this day, inftead of America, to be called Cabotia.

CONTENTS.

Contents.

CHAPTER IX.

Contents.

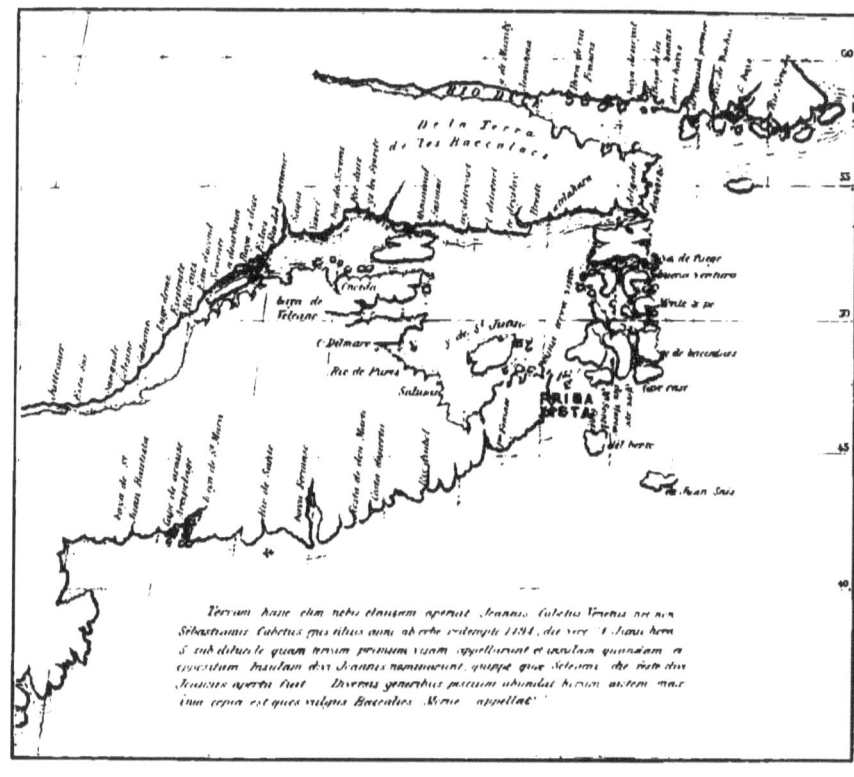

Terram hanc olim nobis clausam aperuit Joannes Cabotus Venetus nec non
Sebastianus Cabotus eius filius anno ab orbe redempto 1494, die vero 24 Junii hora
5 sub diluculo te quam terram primum visam appellarunt et insulam quandam ei
oppositam Insulam divi Joannis nominarunt, quippe quae Solemni die festo divi
Joannis aperta fuit. Diversis generibus piscium abundat horum autem max
ima copia est quos vulgus Baccalaos Moni appellat.

Sebastian Cabot Captain and Filot Major of His Sacred Imperial
Majesty the Emperor Don Carlos the 5 of this name and King our Lord,
made this figure extended in plane in the year of the birth of our
Saviour Jesus Christ 1544

LIFE OF SEBASTIAN CABOT.

CHAPTER I.

The Fifteenth Century a time of awakening and difcovery. Printing acceffory to, and a quickener of, Maritime energy. Firft beginning of the Oriental trade, until its abforption by the Venetians.

HE clofing decades of the fifteenth century form one of the turning points of the world's hiftory. Darknefs had covered the earth, and thick darknefs had mantled around its people; but now it began to feel the folid land; to emerge from the mire of ignorance and fu-perftition in which it had long been floundering, and to difcern, though as yet but dimly, in the grey dawning light, the mifty path of its future travel.

That mighty difcovery, printing, was like a new creation, and God's fiat, " Light BE !" was as potent in the world of intellect as it erft was in the world of matter.

The buried treafure of the ancients was now exhumed; the garnered ftore of the gathered wifdom of the bygone ages, hitherto inacceffible, was unlocked, and the living feed, fcattered over the globe, gladdened its inhabitants, enlarging and enriching their minds, and was hailed with rapture by all who valued learning.

The early printers were either fcholars themfelves, or they kept learned men in their employment to revife and correct each fheet as it came from the prefs.

Hence, books were at firft luxuries in which only popes, emperors, and kings could indulge.

The firft object of the printers was rather to diffufe the accumulated learning of the paft, than to difcover and develope new mines of intellect in the living age ; earneftly they fet themfelves to the tafk of refcuing the fcattered manufcripts of the orators, hiftorians, poets

and philoſophers of Greece and Rome from
oblivion; and ſoon placed theſe beyond the
riſk of extinction from neglect or ignorant
careleſſneſs.

As ſoon as the princes and public libraries, **Great demand for books.**
&c., were ſupplied, the craving deſires of men
of letters, but of limited means, elicited cheaper
editions, which reduced at once the coſtly and
cumbrous folio to the compact neat octavo or
duodecimo.

Very ſoon the printer found there was a
market for his wares in the Univerſities, large
towns, and amongſt at leaſt a portion of the
country gentry and clergy, who conſtantly demanded cheaper editions of the early claſſics.

This demand opened, widened, and deepened
the fountains of literature. Scholarly printers,
like Aldus, no longer waited for the approving
nod of pope, emperor, or cardinal, ere they
began to print; and with a regular and
increaſing demand, ſervile dependence on great
patrons died out.

Brought now into colliſion with the mighty
dead, the living intellect hitherto " cabined,
cribbed, confined," began to germinate;

thoughts, vague and undefined, which had been floating about in their own minds, ftudents found had prefented themfelves, perhaps in a different phafe, to others; or the ftudy of books, gave to them the proof that had been wanting in their own experience, and forthwith, as Minerva fprung ready armed from the head of Jove, the theorem was complete and they rufhed into print.

Then daring, practical men arofe, who reduced the theory to practice, and amidft a multitude, doubtlefs, of ftillborn failures, the world was conftantly aroufed by the tidings of fome new and brilliant fuccefs.

Reformation.

Coincident with the difcovery of the new art, and running parallel with its progrefs, if not heading and leading it, came the doctrines of the Reformation, which proclaimed the Bible as the all-fufficient and only infallible teacher of man.

This, meeting a felt want, and promifing to fill an aching, empty void in the human heart, at once created a clamorous demand for the word of God.

The Dame Partingtons of the day ftrove in

vain to ſtem the tide; buying up the early tomes and burning them, they unwittingly advertiſed and found capital for new and more correct editions, ſo that in ſeventy-four years, from A.D. 1526 to A.D. 1600, we had in England alone 326 editions of the Bible, or parts of the Bible, printed, and theſe were not a tithe of the whole, for the preſſes of Europe were teeming with the ſcriptures.

Bible, numbers printed in England.

Printing had no inconſiderable influence on the pioneers of geographical diſcovery.

Geographical diſcovery ſtimulated.

They found that Diodorus Siculus deſcribed certain Carthaginian ſailors who had voyaged through the pillars of Hercules into the Atlantic Ocean, and there diſcovered a country which furniſhed all the neceſſaries and conveniences of life.

That the Phœnicians, Greeks and Sataſpes the Perſian, had coaſted Africa, whilſt Parmenides had, ages on ages before, divided the earth into zones.

That Ptolemy, in the ſecond century, had applied geometrical principles to the conſtruction of maps, the different projections of the ſphere, and had alſo diſtributed the places of

Ptolemy.

the earth according to their feveral latitudes and longitudes.

Well fatisfied that the earth was a fphere, they fought a fhort cut to Cathay, or the Eaft Indies, undeterred though not unappalled, by the real or imaginary dangers which they fuppofed to be in the way; for the early geographers had pictured the Occident as the home of demons of horrid form, and their maps briftled with figures which, in that fuperftitious age, were enough to terrify all but a few true-hearted noble minds.

Early terrors of Navigation.

Thefe, rifing themfelves above the fear of fpiritual hobgoblins, had not only to calm the terrors of their followers and encourage the timid, but alfo to devife plans for overcoming the real phyfical dangers which befet their unknown pathway.

Iceland.

Iceland (then fpelt Ifland) had been known and was a place of trade for Briftol merchants. Columbus vifited it and failed into a high northern latitude ere he fought employment with Spain; but, between it and the longfought defired haven, floated huge fields or towering bergs of ice, which deterred the timid

or hindered the ambitious mariner, who ſought
to get to the eaſt by ſailing due weſt.

The central zone was equally well guarded
by what is now known as the Sarguſſum Sea,
a vaſt belt of floating ſeaweed which covers an
extent of ocean equal in ſize to the Mediterranean Sea.

The ſouth-weſt and north-weſt ſeemed alone
to afford a ſolution of the difficulty, and to offer
a ſhorter road to the attainment of their objeét.

Let us briefly conſider how the oriental trade
had grown and been carried on.

From before the eighth century Conſtantinople had drawn rich ſtores from the Indies,
and that metropolis of the eaſtern empire had,
notwithſtanding the diſadvantages attendant on
a long and perilous overland route for this
traffic, acquired and retained the poſition of
the opulent mart for the produce of Cathay.

Antioch and Tyre, whoſe ſhips coaſted along
the ſhores of the Perſian Gulf and the Red
Sea, ſuccefsfully competed for their ſhare in
the riches of the Orient.

When the Croiſaders, on their way to the
Holy Land, viewed the magnificence and ſplen-

Conſtan-
tinople, ſeat
of the Indian
trade.

dour which Conftantinople and the other cities
that they captured had attained through being
the channels for the trade, they fet to work to
learn the arts and to fathom the policy of their
inhabitants: they traced the fources of their
wealth, and as long as they held any poft in
the country they encouraged this long-efta-
blifhed commerce.

Venice and
Genoa take
to the trade.
Keen-fighted practical men, fuch as the
Venetians and Genoefe traders and merchants
were, whofe country had been benefited and
their large wealth amaffed by thefe holy wars,
gradually crept into, and ere long engroffed
nearly the whole of this Indian trade.

Precious commodities of fmall bulk, as
cloves, nutmegs, pearls and diamonds, were
long carried viâ the Perfian Gulf, Buffora and
Bagdad, to fome port on the Mediterranean;
whilft more bulky goods came by the Red
Sea and through Alexandria.

Conftant robberies by the land route and a
Egyptian tri-
bute.
heavy tribute by the fea, levied in Egypt, kept
the prices fo high, that it is really wonderful
how buyers could be found; neverthelefs the
demand fteadily increafed.

The wily Mohammedans took care to keep the producer and conſumer aſunder; no Chriſtian was allowed to paſs through their countries to trade direét with the Indies; (by the general term Indies, will be underſtood all thè iſlands and countries eaſt of the Perſian Gulf).

By-and-by came the dreadful incurſions of the Tartars, under "Jenghis Khan," who broke up the power of the Mohammedans.

Through the thus ſcattered tribes an adventurous brave Venetian, Marco Paulo by name, in the thirteenth century reached Bengal, Guzerat, China and Pekin; viſited Java, Ceylon, and Malabar; to all of which he gave the names they now bear; he mentions alſo, though he did not viſit it, the Iſle of Zipangri, moſt probably a part of Japan.

The diſcovery of theſe immenſe regions, hitherto unviſited, of mythical extent, the fabulous accounts of their wealth, furniſhed room for ſpeculation and ſtimulated adventure.

The trade ſteadily increaſed for two centuries. Then came the irruption of the Saracens, and, finally, their capture of Conſtantinople in 1453 A.D., which at once threw the

Marginal notes:

Tartar incurſions.

Marco Paulo's travels. He returned, A. D. 1291, immenſely rich. See Iſaacſon's "Saturni Ephemerides," `A. D. 1635.

Saracens take Conſtantinople.

whole trade into the hands of the Venetians, through the foreſight with which they had ſecured a road by a treaty with Egypt in 1425, A.D.

Their great rivals, the Genoeſe, had cultivated the trade with Greece and Conſtantinople, getting their ſupplies thence, and having large

Genoa crippled, A. D. 1453.

eſtabliſhments there; but they were now driven from theſe poſſeſſions by the Turks, and ſo thoroughly humbled that they could no longer contend with the Queen of the Adriatic.

CHAPTER II.

*Venetian policy; growth in riches; caufes of her decay.
Reputed difcovery of Brazil in* A.D. 1460, *by a citizen
of Nuremberg. Columbus. John Cabot's advent in
England; fettlement at Briftol; probable fite of his
home; poffibility of his having been an Englifhman;
acquires his citizenfhip in Venice in* A.D. 1476;
Sebaftian born in Briftol about 1472, A.D. *Henry VII.'s
firft Charter to the family.*

HE crafty Venetians did not, like
their predeceffors, drain Europe
of its gold and filver to pay for
the commodities they bought, but,
purchafing of the merchants in Egypt and
Syria, they paid them by barter; taking to
them the produce of Europe in exchange, and
thus making a profit both ways.

Venice now became the emporium for Indian goods, and attained fuch power and
fplendour as never .before, or feldom fince,

belonged to any European ftate; their magnificent houfes, rich furniture, profufion of
plate, and elegance of living, furpaffed conception.

Nor was this mere oftentatious difplay, but
the natural refult of fuccefsful induftry, which,
having with eafe acquired wealth, chofe to enjoy it in fplendour.

To carry on the trade the nobles and rich
merchants lent their moneys, at a good rate of
intereft, in the eleventh century getting 20 per
cent., and even down to the fifteenth they made
regularly their 12 per cent. on fuch tranf-
actions.

In addition to the commerce thus opened
up, and now monopolized by Venice, fhe, all
but fingle-handed, withftood on the feaboard
the advance of the encroaching, invading
Saracens or Turks, not only repaying her
expenfes, but enriching herfelf with the fpoils
of the cities fhe captured.

Tapeftries which Grecian dames, like Pe-
nelope, had woven, were ruthlefsly torn from
the walls; Damafcene blades, richly inlaid
yataghans, paintings, and fculpture, found

their way to Venice, and the city laboured under a plethora of wealth.

At laſt, about A. D. 1470, the tide of victory ſeemed to turn; the Turks entered and overran Dalmatia and Auſtria, carrying away 5000 captives; laid waſte Boſnia, Styria, Carinthia, took Capha, Taurica, Cherſomreſus, doing very great damage to the Venetian territories, ſo that in 1478 the Republic was glad to make peace.

Two years after this Venice joined the Florentines in a war againſt the Pope, in which, in two years, ſhe ſpent 600,000 crowns.

Wars and rumours of war in quick ſucceſſion follow, until we are not ſurpriſed to find the Turk again overrunning her territories, and taking 4000 of her people captive on one occaſion.

Lepanto, Medona, Crotone, Pilas and Ciſſeum ſuccumbed before the invader; the Saracen found firm footing in Italy, and Venice was again glad to make peace with Bajazat.

Meanwhile two heavier blows than even

Turks ſucceſsful.

A. D. 1502.

thefe expenfive wars, were being dealt to the
queenly city. We take the fecond of thefe
firft.

After a tedious courfe of voyages, Vafco
De Gama de Gama doubled the Cape of Good Hope,
doubles the and coafted fuccefsfully the weftern fhores of
Cape. Africa, reaching Calicut, on the Malabar
coaft, on the 24th May, 1498, A. D.

Loading his fhip with the produce of that
country, and of the more remote regions which
he found there, he efcaped a multitude of
dangers, and returned fafely to Portugal.

Here he had a moft gracious reception, and
the king at once fecured by papal bull the
fole right to trade with the new lands thus
vifited, which were, in fact, treated as new
difcoveries by Portugal.

This was a mortal ftab to the trade of
Venice, from which it never recovered.

The other blow, though in reality firft
ftruck, was more flow, but even more certain,
and juft as fatal in its operation.

As long fince as A. D. 1460 (fo the archives
of Nuremberg ftate) one of their citizens,
Behem. Martin Behem by name, had failed in queft

of the mythical land diſcovered in the Atlantic by the Carthaginians.

He reached Madeira, and founding a colony of Flemings there was by the king of Portugal made governor of Fayal, and in 1484, in ſhips provided by the king, he, it is ſaid, diſcovered Brazil, and even the ſtraits now known by the name of Magellan.

His own letters, a terreſtrial globe, and charts of the lands thus diſcovered, arc ſaid to have been depoſited in 1492, and are ſtill preſerved in the archives of his native city. Hartman Schedl, and Petreus Matreus, writing two years before the diſcoveries of Columbus, confirm this. It would be exceedingly intereſting to have this verified, but our decided opinion is that he merely drew on his map the theory which Columbus afterwards practically carried out, and we very much doubt the correctneſs of the date 1460. This chart is ſaid to have determined Magellan in the courſe he purſued.

Authors agree that Columbus had ſome information reſpecting the weſtern ſhores, though they all ſpeak very vaguely as to its ſource;

Globe and Charts at Nuremberg.

Columbus.

Hears of the Weſt.

now if this Behem was governor of Fayal during the feveral voyages Columbus made to the Madeiras, the myftery is, we think, explained.

Nor does it detract from the honours due to Columbus, for Behem does not feem to have thought that he had found more than an ifland, and that not one of the rich Indies fo ardently defiderated.

Difcovers Weft Indies. Columbus, when at laft he got a chance, took a more northerly courfe than Behem; and whilft he really found iflands—and very rich ones—even he never dreamt of a continent fo near at hand, of which, be it remembered, he never faw the fhores until Auguft 1498, A.D.

This difcovery of the central part of America Spain, her wealth. put Spain into poffeffion of immenfe treafures, which were gradually diffufed over Europe.

Thefe ftimulated the induftry of other nations, and made them exert themfelves in fuch a way as foon to leffen the demand for the Eaftern goods through the expenfive channel of Venice.

There a gradual decline of trade had, from

the middle of the century, neceſſitated a more diſtant ſearch for cuſtomers. " If the mountain would not come to Mahomet, Mahomet muſt go to the mountain."

From this cauſe, probably, about 1460 or 1470, John Cabot, who it is expreſsly ſaid " came to London to follow the trade of merchandize," found his way to Briſtol, the ſecond city in the kingdom, and containing, as we ſhall by-and-by ſee, at leaſt ſome congenial and brotherly adventurous ſpirits.

John Cabot ſettles at Briſtol.

In this city, not being allowed, by exiſting jealous charters, which preſcribed that no ſtranger tradeſman ſhould dwell in or tarry in the town for the ſale of his wares beyond forty days, he could find no reſting place.

" Carta Johannis Comitis Moreton, A. D. 1188, afterwards King John, alſo 36 Henry III. 1252 A.D., alſo 28 Edward I. 1300 A.D., &c.&c."

He would moſt likely then ſettle in the ſuburb neareſt to the town and ſhipping. Thoſe on the north and weſt were already occupied by the Jews (Jacob's Wells and Stonebridge), between whom and the Venetians there was no congeniality of feeling.

The eaſtern ſuburb lay too far from the river, ſo that there was only the ſouthern left; and Langmead and Lokeings Croft, now known as Cathay, running right up under the very fhadow of old St. Mary Redcliffe Church, would, to the foreigner, compelled to live and trade outfide the bounds of the city, offer the moft convenient fite.

Cathay, a Briftol fuburb.

Doubtlefs, other Venetians traded here alfo, and their goods being moftly from Cathay, as the Indies were called, we may fairly fuppofe gave the locality the defignation which it bears to this day.

Tradition fays Sebaftian was born here.

Here then it is probable John Cabot fettled (and traded), having for a fhort period as a near neighbour, on the other fide of the church, the famous William Canynge. May we not conjecture alfo that the wealthy Englifh merchant and the rich Venetian trader ftruck hands at many a bargain, and drank not a few tankards of fpiced Canary together? Somewhere in this locality his two younger fons, Sebaftian and Sanctus, were born; for though we know what Sebaftian is reported to have told Contarini, the plain fimple words of his utterance to R. Eden are fo natural and truthful, that we at once accept them, and will deal with the other ftatement elfewhere. Eden fays, then (fol. 255):

Eden, fol. 255.

" Sebaſtian Cabot told me that he was borne
in Bryſtowe, and that at iiij yeare ould he was
carried with his father to Venice, and ſo returned agayne into England with his father
after certayne years, whereby he was thought
to have been born in Venice."

Here we have the queſtion ſettled more
than three hundred years ſince, on the higheſt
authority, as to the city of his birth ; the date
is not ſo eaſily fixed, different writers placing
it from about A.D. 1474 to A.D. 1477.

We are much inclined, for ſeveral reaſons,
to adopt the firſt date as the neareſt the truth.
Richard Eden, in his " Decades of the New
World,"&c. (A.D. 1555), ſpeaking of him as one
knowing him intimately, does ſo in language
which implies great age. One chapter has for
its title, " Lykewyſe of the vyages of that
woorthy man, Sebaſtian Cabote, yat lyvynge,"
&c. But the matter is now, we think, ſatiſ-
factorily ſettled by Rawdon Brown's " Venetian Calendar," taken from the Archives of
Venice, where, under date of Auguſt 11,
1472, is a privilege conferring the rights of
citizenſhip on Aloiſe Fontano, of Bergame,

and a fupplementary memorandum, purport-
ing that fixteen other privileges, of later date,
had been conceded to various individuals, including one to John Cabot, thus: "Simile
privilegium faftum fuit Johanni Caboot fub
duce fupra fcripto, A.D. 1476."

John Cabot
made a citi-
zen of Venice
1476, "Ve-
netian Calen-
dar."

Under date March 29, 1476, we find a
decree of the Senate, "That a privilege of
citizenfhip, within and without, be made for
John Cabot, as ufual, for a refidence of fifteen
years. Ayes, 149. Noes, 0. Neutral, 0."

This proves John to have been in Venice
in 1476. Sebaftian fays that he was four years

Born in 1472.

old when taken there, which places his birth in
1472. If, however, John arrived in Venice and
fued out a patent in A.D. 1472, which was not completed until 1476, when he was again leaving—
and the two entries may mean this—this would
then place Sebaftian's birth as early as A.D. 1468.

Sebaftian
Cabot old
enough to
command
in 1497.

However, the proof feems conclufive that
he was at the leaft twenty-three years of age
at the date of the firft patent of 1495, and
confequently was twenty-five at the failing of
the expedition and the landing on the American continent in 1497.

This removes an objection which ſome have hazarded as to Sebaſtian's extreme youth, and the improbability of his being employed in ſo hazardous a work.

We muſt remember alſo that Venice and Genoa largely ſupplied us with ſailors as well as ſhips, and all Sebaſtian's after life proved that he was the peer of Columbus himſelf in the ſcience of navigation, and his moſt worthy ſucceſſor in the office of Grand Pilot to the Court of Spain.

Trained with firſt rate ſai-lors.

Such a manhood would have had a promiſ-ing youth; the future ſeaman muſt have been plainly diſcoverable between the age of ſeven-teen and twenty-five—the two extremes given as to his age at the date of the firſt voyage.

What countryman originally was John Ca-bot? As we have ſeen, he only becomes a Venetian citizen in 1476. Was old John Stow right in calling him a Genoeſe, or was he after all an Engliſhman, who for ſome ſer-vice had this honour conferred upon him, even as William Gold had? For aught that ap-pears to the contrary, he himſelf might have been born in Briſtol; and not many years

What coun-tryman was John Cabot?

Wm. Gold, ſee " Vene-tian Calen-dar," a brave Engliſh ad-venturer.

since we are assured there were several deeds
in the muniment chest of St. Thomas, in this
city, of Henry VII.'s reign, which were at-
tested by some of that name. Unfortunately,
and though most diligent search has been made
after them, it has been hitherto unsuccefsful.

Ere we leave this part of the subject, let us
observe, that in the first patent the name
of his youngest brother, Sanctus, is also mentioned. This, we think, affords strong cor-
roboration, if not absolute proof, that the age
of Sebaftian was greater than many of his
biographers have supposed, for it is not very
likely that a minor's name would be associated
in a King's patent.

Further, though it is said of him that he
returned, when a youth, from Venice to England, it is nowhere said that this patent of
1495 was granted immediately on his arrival;
he may probably have been here for years.

" His early voyages foftered in him a love
for the fea, and from boyhood he was inftructed
in all the known branches of navigation; he
thus became an apt scholar in the profefion
he loved, and made several short trips to fea,

in order to acquire a practical as well as theo-
retical knowledge."

At the probable period of his return to his
native place, Europe was ringing with the difcoveries of Columbus, and Henry VII., full
of chagrin that through his own parfimony
and delay he had loft the prize which Spain
had won, had concluded a treaty with Denmark, by which he could pour into Iceland
(Iſland) all kinds of clothing, proviſions or
other commodities, without let or hindrance,
evidently (and probably by the elder Cabot's
advice) aiming to make it a fort of half-way
houfe in the north-weft road to Cathay.

Sebaftian Cabot, full of enthufiafm, does
full juftice to the mafter-mind of the feas;
and fpeaking of the difcoveries of Columbus,
fays: "All men with great admiration affirm
it to be more divine than human: the fame
and report thereof increafed in my heart a
great flame and defire to attempt fome notable
thing."

And being, Stow fays, "expert with knowledge of the circuit of the world, and the
iſlands of the fame, as by his charts and other

Marginal notes:

Returning from his voyages, he hears of the fame of Columbus.

Henry VII. concludes a treaty for trading with Iceland.

Cabot praifes and feeks to emulate Columbus.

Stow's "Annals," p. 804, ed. 1605 A.D.

reasonable demonstrations he showed, caused the King to man and victual a ship," &c.

The charter shows this to have been an error. The rich Venetian merchant and his sons were to find the ship and bear all expenses, the wily king stipulating for one-fifth of the gains, without any risk whatever.

The patent runs thus :—

Henry VII.'s
first Charter
to the Cabot
family for
five ships.

" Henry, by the grace of God, &c. &c.

" Be it known to all, that we have given and granted, and by these presents do give and grant, to our well-beloved John Cabot, citizen of Venice, to Lewis, Sebastian, and Sanctus, sons of the said John, and to their heirs and deputies, full and free authority, leave and power, to sail to all parts, countries and seas of the *East*, of the *West*, and of the North, under our banners and ensigns, with five ships, of what burthen or quality soever they be, and as many mariners and men as they will take with them in the said ships, *upon their own proper costs and charges*, to seek out, discover and find, whatsoever Isles, Countries, Regions or Provinces of the Heathen and Infidels, whatsoever they be, and in whatsoever part of

the world which before this time have been
unknown to all Chriſtians. We have granted
to them and every of them and their deputies,
and have given them our licenſe, to ſet up our
banners and enſigns in every village, town,
caſtle, iſle or mainland, of them newly found;
and that the ſaid John and his ſons and their
heirs may ſubdue, occupy and poſſefs all ſuch
towns, cities, &c. by them found, which they
can ſubdue, occupy and poſſefs as our vaſſals
and lieutenants, getting to us the rule, title
and juriſdiction of the ſaid villages, towns, &c.

" Yet ſo that the ſaid John and his ſons and
their heirs, of all the fruits, profits and commodities growing from ſuch navigation, ſhall
be held and bound to pay to us, in wares or
money, the *fifth part of the capital gain* ſo
gotten for every their voyage, as often as they
ſhall arrive at our port of Briſtol (at which
port they ſhall be obliged only to arrive), de-
ducting all manner of neceſſary coſts and
charges by them made: we giving and granting unto them and their heirs and deputies
that they ſhall be free from all payments of
cuſtoms on all ſuch merchandize they ſhall

To conquer,
occupy, pof-
fefs, trade,
and pay the
king, in wares
or money,
one fifth of
of the net
profit at Brif-
tol each voy-
age.

bring with them from the places ſo newly
found.

None other
to trade thi-
ther on pain
of forfeiture
of ſhips and
goods.

" And moreover we have given and granted
to them and their heirs and deputies that all
the firm land, iſlands, villages, towns, &c.
they ſhall chance to find, may not, without
licenſe of the ſaid John Cabot and his ſons, be
ſo frequented and viſited, under pain of loſing
their ſhips and all the goods of them who
ſhall preſume to ſail to the places ſo found.

" Willing, and commanding ſtrictly all and
ſingular our ſubjects, as well on land as on
ſea, to give good aſſiſtance to the ſaid John

The Cabots
find the
money.

and his ſons and deputies, and that as well in
arming and furniſhing their ſhips and veſſels
as in proviſion of food and buying victuals for
their money, and all other things by them to
be provided neceſſary for the ſaid navigation,
they do give them all their favours and aſſiſtance.

" Witneſs myſelf at Weſtminſter, 5th March,
in the eleventh year of our reign, or 1495 A.D."
As the civil year began on March 25th this
would be really in the year 1496 A.D., one year
only before the expedition ſailed.

CHAPTER III.

Hypothetical voyage of the Cabots, in 1474 A. D., *previous to the Charter of Henry ; fupported by Sebaſtian Cabot's Map, publiſhed* 1544, *now in Paris: reaſons which ſtrengthen this view. State of England, and of Briſtol, at the period of the Charter.*

HE foregoing is the original charter of Henry VII., which is generally ſuppoſed to have preceded the diſcovery. A contrary theory has been broached, and is upheld by Harris, Pinkerton, Barrow, and others; viz., that the Cabots had, from their own private reſources, ſailed weſtward, and, diſcovering the land, returned haſtily, and, by their repreſentations induced the king to grant them this patent. The two firſt named write as follows :—

" But the year before that patent was granted, viz., in 1494, John Cabot, with his ſon Sebaſtian, had ſailed from Briſtol upon diſcovery,

Theory of an earlier voyage.

Harris, vol. ii. p. 190, ed. 1744.

and had actually feen the continent of Newfoundland, to which they gave the name of
'Prima Vifta,' or firft feen. And on the 24th
of June in the fame year, he went on fhore on
an ifland, which, becaufe it was difcovered on
that day, he called 'St. John's;' and of this
ifland he reported very truly that the foil was
barren, that it yielded little, and that the people
wear bearfkin clothes and were armed with
bows, arrows, pikes, darts, wooden clubs, and
flings; but that the coaft abounded with fifh,
and upon this report of his, the before-men-
tioned patent of March 5, 1496, was granted."
Herein is the record of all the voyages mud-
dled up in one ftatement.

Barrow,
"Chronolo-
gical Hiftory
of Voyages,"
p. 32.

Barrow fays, "there is no poffible way of
reconciling the various accounts but by fuppofing John Cabot to have made one voyage,
at leaft, previous to the date of the patent,
and fome time between that and the date of
the return of Columbus, either in 1494 or
1495."

Now, the above ftatements agree entirely
with the infcription on the map of Seb. Cabot

See Map.

in the "Bibliotheque Imperial" of Paris, date

1544, publiſhed during Cabot's lifetime, which is as follows :—

"Terram hanc olim nobis clauſam aperuit Johannes Cabotus Venetus, nec non Sebaſtianus Cabotus ejus filius anno ab orbe redempto, 1494, die vero 24 Junii hora 5, ſub dilucolo quam terram primum viſam appellârunt et inſulam quandam ei oppoſitam Inſulam divi Joannis nominârunt quippe quæ ſolemni die feſto divi Joannis aperte fuit."

Only en-graven map of Cabot's in exiſtence at " Bibliotheque Imperial," Paris.

This inſcription cannot be a miſtake in the date, for it is alike in both the Spaniſh and the Latin inſcriptions, and it is abundantly evident that the publiſher of the map conſidered and believed it to be perfectly true that Cabot did make this voyage in 1494. Kochhaf alſo notes this date in his book as having been ſeen by him on a map of Cabot at Oxford.

Kochhaf's teſtimony.

By the courteſy of the officials connected with the above admirable library, and the kindneſs of R. H. Major, Eſq., F.S.A., of the map department of the Britiſh Muſeum, we are enabled to give a fac ſimile of this precious document ; "The only engraven copy," ſays Monſieur Taſchereau, "which is known of the map of

Sebaftian Cabot." If, therefore, this is to be depended on, we muft antedate the difcovery by three years, and fuppofe, which is probable enough, that immediately on Columbus' return, in March, 1493, as foon as the news fpread, it fired the ambition of the Cabots, and getting ready during the enfuing winter for an adventurous voyage, they ftarted in the early fummer of 1494, and difcovered the land at Cape Breton on June 24, in that year.

Cape Breton probably difcovered firft, and that in 1494.

The above view is perfectly confiftent with Sebaftian's defcription to Ramufio's friend; nor is it at all at variance with the wording of the firft charter, but rather the contrary. "They were to 'take five fhips, to fet up our banner and enfigns in every village, town, caftle, ifle, or mainland of them newly found.' * * * to trade and pay a fifth of the profits to the king."

For an uncertain voyage of difcovery, five fhips would be needlefs: for trading purpofes with a newly-difcovered region as a mutual defence, and a politic difplay of power before the heathen and infidels we can underftand it. Befides, in the Venetian envoy's letter, written after the return from the firſt voyage under the charter, he is ſpoken of as "a man who has good ſkill in diſcovering new iſlands;" a retroſpective view, which points back to ſome diſcovery previous to the one juſt then made.

" Venetian
Calendar."

Again, in the "Spaniſh State Papers," vol. i. p. 177, we have corroborative teſtimony which carries us back actually beyond the date of Columbus. Don Pedro de Ayala, a Spaniſh envoy in England, in a letter to his ſovereigns Ferdinand and Iſabella, dated July 25, 1498, ſays " That the people of Briſtol ſent out every year two or three or four light ſhips, caravelas, in ſearch of the iſland of Brazil and the ſeven cities, according to the fancy of that Italian Cabot, and that they have done for the laſt ſeven years."

Pedro de Ay-
ala, the Spa-
niſh envoy,
ſays Briſtol
and Cabot ſent
out ſhips in
ſearch as early
as 1491, one
year before
Columbus,
vide "Spaniſh
State Papers,"
vol. i. p. 177.

Whether the father or the ſon was the moving ſpirit of the enterpriſe, muſt be left largely to conjecture; one thing ſeems to be quite certain, Lewis and Sanctus, who are named in the patent, did not ſail in the ſhip; it was either John and Sebaſtian, or Sebaſtian alone, to whom the honour of the diſcovery belongs.

Though the charter was granted in 1495, yet from fome unknown reafon, moft probably the difordered ftate of the country, the expedition did not fet fail until early in the fummer of 1497; and then in but one fhip, the now famous "Matthew," of and from Briftol.

It was the cuftom in England (*vide* the "Venetian Calendar") to hire mariners by the voyage; it is not wonderful then, or even matter of furprife to us to find, as we fhall, in the courfe of the narrative, that the men were in a hurry to return, and wifhed to fhorten their perilous fearch as much as poffible.

Venice acted more wifely, paying her failors by the month and inflicting a penalty of 200 ducats on any captain who hired men by the voyage.

It may help us to a better underftanding of the greatnefs of the undertaking, if inftead of looking at it from our ftand point in this year of grace 1869, we fancy ourfelves living in the clofe of the fifteenth century, and, as in a panorama, view the varied pictures it prefents at that period.

Erafmus, in his letters, gives us fome pictureſque peeps at our anceſtor's life, more pungent than pleaſant. He ſays: "The Engliſh conſtruct their rooms ſo as to admit of no thorough draft; before I was thirty years old, if I ſlept in a room which had been ſhut up for months without ventilation, I was immediately attacked with fever."

Jortin's Eraſmus, p. 60.

It was his opinion (and a moſt ſenſible one it was) that the impure atmoſphere of the dwellings cauſed the deadly peſtilence called the "ſweating ſickneſs," which broke out about 1486. In Briſtol it carried off vaſt numbers of the inhabitants; both here and all over the country, gentle as well as ſimple fell victims.

MS. Calendars.

Evans' "Hiſtory of Briſtol."

Thoſe attacked moſtly died in about three hours: and many towns loſt half their inhabitants.

Strangers were ſaid to be free from danger: was it, perchance, becauſe of their greater perſonal cleanlineſs? for whilſt the houſes of the Engliſh gentry were in the ſtate deſcribed by Eraſmus, we cannot conceive that any claſs of the community were cleanly in their perſons.

Hear what the ſcholar from Rotterdam ſays:

Seyer, vol. ii. p. 205, ſays, in London two mayors and four aldermen died of it. It laſted little more than a month.

Jortin's Eraſ-
mus.
"The dirt, of even the better claſs houſes, is
abominable; the floors are moſtly of clay,
ſtrewed with ruſhes; freſh ruſhes are periodi-
cally laid over them, but the old ones remain
as a foundation for perhaps twenty years together, amidſt which lies, unmoleſted, an ancient
collection of beer, greaſe, fragments, bones,
ſpittle, excrements of dogs and cats, and everything naſty!"

What wonder that in towns crowded with
ſuch homes, peſtilence was ſo frequent and
ſo deadly. The ſame keen obſerver ſays
alſo :—

" It would contribute more to the health of
the people if they ate and drank leſs, and lived
more on freſh meat than ſalt."

The city feaſts were as magnificent in the
days of Henry VII. as they are now, and quite
Capello's "Ita-
lian Relationof
the Iſland of
England," p.
22.
as ſtupid. Franceſco Capello, the Venetian
ambaſſador here in 1502, ſays in his relation
of England : " At the Lord Mayor's banquet
in the Guildhall a thouſand people were ſeated
at table, and the dinner laſted four hours!"

At the ſheriffs' dinner, he ſpeaks alſo of the
infinite profuſion of victuals, and notices " how

punctiliouſly they ſat in their order, and the extraordinary ſilence of every one."

" They think no greater honour can be con- Ibid. p. 22. ferred or received, than to invite others to eat with them ; they would ſooner ſpend five or ſix ducats to provide an entertainment for a perſon, than a groat to aſſiſt him in diſtreſs."

" They have alſo," ſays he, " the incredible courteſy of remaining with their heads un- covered, with an admirable grace, whilſt they talk to each other."

Before leaving this part of our ſubject we will give a bill of the feaſt of one of the arch- biſhops of the land, originally publiſhed in a memoir of the Rev. Dr. Standfaſt, chaplain to Charles I. and rector of Chriſtchurch in the city of Briſtol. The original account was then in the Tower of London.

" George Nevill, brother to the great Earl Briſtol " Chro- nicle," Aug. 9, 1760. of Warwick, on his inſtalment into his arch- biſhoprick of York in the year 1470, made a feaſt for the nobility, gentry and clergy, where he ſpent :—

300 qrs. of Wheat.	104 ton of Wine.
300 ton of Ale.	1 pipe ſpiced Wine.

80 fat Oxen.
6 wild Bulls.
300 Pigs.
1004 Wethers.
300 Hogs.
300 Calves.
3000 Geese.
3000 Capons.
100 Peacocks.
200 Cranes.
200 Kids.
2000 Chicken.
4000 Pigeons.
4000 Rabbits.
204 Bitterns.
4000 Ducks.
400 Hernsies.
200 Pheasants.
500 Partridges.

400 Woodcocks.
4400 Plovers.
100 Curlews.
100 Quails.
1000 Egrets.
1200 Rees.[1]
4000 Bucks, Does, and
       Roebucks.
155 Hot Venison pasties.
1000 dishes of jellies.
4000 Cold Venison pasties.
2000 Hot Custards.
4000 Cold   do.
400 Tarts.
300 Pike.
300 Bream.
8 Seals.
4 Porpusses.

At this feast the Earl of Warwick was steward; the Earl of Bedford, treasurer; the Lord Hastings, comptroller; with many noble officers, servitors.

---

[1] Rees. *Sic.* orig. ♀. is this the female of the Ruff, Ruffs and Reeves?

     " Her olives with her wyn trees
     These foxes brent with her rees."
—*Curson Mundie MSS.* Trin. Coll. Camb. f. 45.

There were 1000 cooks.

62 kitcheners.

515 ſcullions."

Whether feaſting, ſuch as above deſcribed, and a taſte for ſuch unctuous delicacies as "ſeals and porpuſſes" be a virtue or not, moſt people will allow patriotiſm to be an undoubted one.

Our national pride is not a thing of yeſterday. Eraſmus ſays :

"Above all things, take care not to cenſure or deſpiſe any individual things in the country; the natives are very patriotic, and not without reaſon."

Eraſmus' Letter, 1527.

Grocyne, a Briſtol man, was one of Eraſmus' moſt intimate friends in this country, and was the firſt public profeſſor of the Greek tongue at Oxon when the great foreigner was there, who in his epiſtles owns him "pro patrono ſuo et preceptore." We may be pretty well ſure that the Briſtol man then, even as now, would ſtand up for his country, and, "not without reaſon."

Grocyne of Briſtol. Firſt public Greek Profeſſor at Oxford.

Capello alſo ſays: "They think there are no other men but themſelves, and no other world but England; and whenever they ſee a

Italian relation.

handſome foreigner, they ſay he looks like an Engliſhman."

Good, quaint old John Stow, the tailor, who, thank God, forſook his profeſſion and turned antiquary—(though he had, it is ſaid, in conſequence, to ſtand and beg at the church doors for his living) ſays:—

Stow's " Survey of London," ed. 1633, p. 84. " On feſtival days and the vigils of feſtival days, after the ſun-ſetting, there were generally made bonfires in the ſtreets, every man beſtowing wood and labour towards them; the wealthier, before their doors, near to theſe fires, would ſet out tables with ſweet bread and good drink plentifully; whereto they would invite their neighbours and paſſengers alſo, to ſit and be merry with them in great familiarity, praiſing God for the benefits beſtowed on them."

Bacon, p. 242. Henry VII. exhibits himſelf repeatedly in the charaᵈer of a royal ſwindler, on the teſtimony of Lord Bacon; and certainly ſome very queer laws were in force.

11th Henry VII. cap. 8. One, during his reign, enaᵈed that " Any one lending money for a time and taking anything for the ſaid loan ſhould loſe one half of the money he had lent."

Another forbad coin, bullion or jewels, to be carried out of the realm above a certain ſum, and our good friend Eraſmus himſelf, with his hard-earned and well-won £20 in gold, was ſtopped at Dover and all his money but the allowed ſum of ſix angels, was taken from him.

4th Henry VII. cap. 23.

Laycey's Jorlin, p. 13.

It is therefore evident that the capital of the country was hoarded. " The king died worth £1,800,000, an enormous ſum in thoſe days."

Bacon, and " Excerpta Hiſtorica."

Capello ſays again, " The viſible wealth of the people was the admiration of foreigners (it had migrated from Venice by this time, 1502); the ſmall innkeepers ſerved you on ſilver diſhes, with ſilver tankards, and each tavern, however humble, would contain £100 worth of ſilver plate."

Italian relation pp. 29, 42.

In Briſtol, vagrants were ſet to work in priſon ; thieves were proſecuted without mercy ; yet never was murder and robbery ſo rife before or ſince.

Seyer's " Hiſtory of Briſtol."

The cucking-ſtool in the ditch under the caſtle walls was uſed for fraudulent brewers, and diſhoneſt bakers were dragged through the town on a ſledge (with their falſe ſcales,

Briſtol Charter, Edward III. 24th April, 1347.

&c., fufpended over their heads), to be pelted as in the pillory.

The old city was mainly confined to the area between the two rivers, and Temple, Thomas, and Redcliff, which three parifhes were bounded by a wall and moat that ran from St. John's Lane, Redcliff Hill, through Portwall Lane and Temple Gate to the Tower Harritz.

All round the city the little hills covered with woods came clofe to its gates ; wild deer, herded in Clifton Wood, whilft the low marfhy lands fkirting the river were frequented by wild fowl.

The tidal waters, innocent of fewage, abounded in fifh, amongft which the filvery falmon, rolling porpoife, and royal fturgeon, held higheft rank.

" Great fhippes in full fail " were borne on the tide right up into the city, and no doubt many a bale of rich goods that never paid duty to the king went in by night at the quaint mullioned windows of the ancient houfes that overhung the old bridge.

From King Street to the Grove was a low flat marfh, where ftood the archery butts, to

which the citizens and their prentices reforted
for practice, alfo for running the quintain,
fword and buckler play, and bowls. The
graver fort promenaded under the trees of
College Green, which, reaching to the Car- **College Green.**
melite Friary on St. Auguſtine's Back (Colſton
Hall), had few buildings thereon fave the mo-
naſtery, and the Hofpital of the Gaunts : there
they liſtened to the fermon preached from the
great ſtone pulpit under the trees in the green,
or watched the progreſs the mafons made in
building the church of St. Auguſtine.

In 1484 a vaſt flood inundated the city and **Great flood,**
drowned over 200 men, women and children. **Oct. 15th
1484.**

Great nobles with their feudal retainers or
friendly neighbours fought pitched battles with
each other, carelefs as to what the king thought
or faid.

One fuch was fought at this period at Nibley **Battle of Nibley Green.**
Green, where Lord Lifle was flain by Thomas
Marquis of Berkeley, Earl Marfhal of England,
whofe next brother, Maurice, afterwards fifth **Maurice, Lord
Berkeley,
marries Philip
Mead's daugh-
ter, who had
great property
at Thornbury.**
earl, had married a daughter of a late mayor
of Briſtol ; and fo the Briſtol men went out
and took part in the fight.

The corporation, as a body, knew how to
enjoy themfelves : juft peep into the Compter
or Tolzey, a kind of open colonnade, called
alfo the Counter, oppofite the High Crofs (or
rather, exactly oppofite the prefent Council
Houfe), where the mayor and fheriff fit daily
from eight till eleven to hear complaints between parties.

But now it is after dinner, on St. Nicholas'
day ; they (the corporation) have dined and
are merry, and while they wait for the coming
of the bifhop, with whom they are going to
St. Nicholas to hear evenfong, they amufe
themfelves by playing at dice, which the worthy
town clerk, R. Ricart, who tells the ftory,
fays he furnifhed at a penny the raffle.

Fancy the learned town clerk handing round
the fets of dice, and the worthy mayor telling
the fheriff to keep his eye open and fee that
the right reverend father does not drop on
them and catch them in the act.

Coming from the "wraftling" with the mayor,
William Vaughan, who had been fheriff, was
killed by a hot-headed Welfh nobleman for
fome fancied flight : perchance he thruft his

tradeſman form betwixt the wind and his nobility.

The principal manufactures of the city were
ſoap, cloth and blankets, which latter were in-
vented by the Brothers Blanket, living in
Tucker Street; where alſo the firſt William
Canning lived, and laid the foundation of the
family's wealth as a cloth manufacturer or
Toucker.

From the parchments recovered from Chat-
terton's mother, and alſo from Barrett the hiſtorian, by Dr. Glyn, we find that " Tapetes,
teſterbed, ſheets and feather pillows (mappas,
table-cloths), manutergia, napkins," &c. which
are ſuppoſed not to have belonged to perſons of
the rank of traders, &c. were not uncommon
in Briſtol, and were repeatedly left by will.

By Dr. Glyn, of Cambridge.

Luxuries of the Briſtol merchants.

There would ſeem, therefore, to have been
more of cleanlineſs and refinement in Briſtol
than Eraſmus met with in Oxford and London.

Theſe are ſome few glimpſes into the ſocial
life and times when Cabot's patent was granted
and his diſcoveries were being made.

CHAPTER IV.

Claims of John, and of Sebaſtian, feverally ſtated, as to the honour of being the firſt diſcoverers. Sebaſtian's portrait; arguments therefrom; his map; reaſons baſed thereon. Hiſtoric evidence and opinions. Additional reaſons given in favour of a previous voyage. The land firſt diſcovered, Nova Scotia, and not Newfoundland. The Iſle of St. John, Prince Edward's Iſland. The voyage of 1497, explored the Gulf of St. Lawrence and the river beyond Quebec; Continent diſcovered fourteen months before Columbus. Return of the expedition.

NOW ariſes the queſtion, as John Cabot's name ſtands firſt in this patent of 1495, and that of 1498 recites his name only, does it neceſſarily follow that he ſailed with this firſt expedition, or was he merely the rich merchant adventurer, whoſe foreſight, money and character eſtabliſhed the adventure and won for it the patronage of the mercenary king?

Many argue that he ſtayed and managed the buſineſs at home; certainly Sebaſtian gives us no hint of his father's preſence in either voyage; but, modeſt, gentle and unaſſuming, as all his life proves him to have been, ſpeaks of the diſcovery ever in the firſt perſon and in the ſingular number.

Our Engliſh hiſtorians ſeem, in this matter, to have been entirely led aſtray by Hakluyt, who, copying from John Stow, perverted the text (thinking it was wrong), and placed the ſkill, talents, and ſeamanſhip of the ſon, to the credit of the father.

Hakluyt, vol. iii. p. 9.

This ſeems to have been done ſimply be-cauſe he found the father's name firſt in the patent of 1495, and ſtanding alone in the pa-tent of 1497, and without the ſlighteſt deſign on the part of the worthy prebendary to injure the fair fame of the ſon.

And juſt as if one ſheep jump the hedge the whole flock follow, ſo have nearly all our naval hiſtorians, copying and enlarging upon Hak-luyt, got further and further from the truth; the tale of the three black crows has been veri-fied in this caſe.

Now look at the two paſſages ſide by ſide:—

Stow, 1605, 1631, and Hakluyt, vol. iii. p. 9.

Stow, A. D. ed. 1605, pp. 804, alſo edit. 1631, pp. 483, ſays :—" This year Sebaſtian Gaboto, a Genoas ſon, born at Briſtol, profeſſing himſelf to be expert in the knowledge of the circuit of the world, and iſlands of the ſame, as by his charts, and other reaſonable demonſtrations he ſhewed," &c. &c.

Hakluyt, profeſſing to copy this, and giving it as his authority, does it thus : —" In the 13 year of King Henry VII., by means of one John Cabot, a Venetian, which made himſelf very expert, and cunning in knowledge of circuit of the world, and iſlands of the ſame. as by a ſea card, and other demonſtrations reaſonable he ſhewed," &c. &c.

Strange to ſay, after making this alteration in the text, Hakluyt retains the original title of the paſſage.

" A note of Sebaſtian Cabot's firſt diſcovery of part of the Indies, taken out of the latter part of Robert Fabyan's Chronicle, not hitherto printed, which is in the cuſtody of Mr. John Stow, a diligent preſerver of antiquities."

An unpubliſhed treatiſe of Hakluyt's, dated 1584, has recently been diſcovered (ſee Wood's Maine Hiſt. Society, 1868), in which he vehemently appeals to the Engliſh government to engage in colonization, and he more than once affirms that the firſt diſcovery was made in 1496, and by Sebaſtian Cabot. " A great part of the continent as well as of the iſlands was firſt diſcovered for the king of England by Sebaſtian Gabote, an Engliſhman, born in Briſtowe, ſon of John Gabote, in 1496 ; naye, more, Gabote diſcovered this large traɗe of firm lande two yeares before Columbus ſaw any part of the continent."

Maine Hiſt. Society, 1868. Hakluyt's heretofore unpubliſhed treatiſe.

We do not ſeek to rob John Cabot of a leaf of his laurels, or detraɗ from his fame ; he was the head of the firm, wiſe and prudent ; and no doubt counſelled his ſon and entered (con amore) into his plans.

It has never been hinted that all of the ſons were engaged in this firſt voyage, but the pre-ſumption is as likely that they, his partners, would do ſo, as that the father, who was now getting into the ſere and yellow leaf, would thus encounter dangers enough to frighten the youthful, and daunt the robuſt.

John Cabot now an old man.

Sir G. Peckham, indeed, as copied by Hak-luyt, ſays : " In the time of the queen's grand-

Sir G. Peck-ham.

Hakluyt, vol.
iii. p. 165.
father, Henry VII., of worthy memory, letters patent were, by his majesty, granted to Sir John Cabota, an Italian; to Lewis, Sebaftian, and Sanctus, his three fons, to difcover remote and barbarous heathen countries, which difcovery was afterwards executed to the ufe of the crown of England in the faid king's time by Sebaftian and Sanctus."

The earlieft Englifh writers on the fubject, as Stow, Willes, Eden, and Sir H. Gilbert, mention Sebaftian as the difcoverer; fo alfo does Sanuto, the Venetian.

Venetian
Calendars.
Thanks to the painftaking and fcholarly refearches of Rawdon Brown, we have now, from the Venetian archives, irrefragable proof that in an expedition from England, under the aufpices of King Henry VII. in the year 1497, the continent was difcovered and taken poffeffion of for England.

A'1g. 24, 1497.
A great dif-
covcrcr of new
iflands previous
to this.
The firft notice is under date Auguft 24, 1497. "Alfo fome months ago his Majefty Henry VII. fent out a Venetian, who is a very good mariner, *and has good fkill in difcovering new iflands*, and he has returned fafe, and has found two very large and fertile new iflands;

having likewiſe diſcovered the ſeven cities,
400 leagues from England, on the weſtern
paſſage. The next ſpring his Majeſty means
to ſend him with fifteen or. twenty ſhips."
(P. 260.)

" Venetian Calendar," p. 260, from the " Sforza Archives."

The Venetian envoy would claſs the ſon as
a Venetian. It may mean one or other, or
both; ſo that the above is quite as applicable
to Sebaſtian as to John.

Where the ſeven cities, 400 leagues from
England, or a little more than half way, could
be, unleſs it was in Iceland, we cannot conjecture.

Ibid.

But we have confeſſedly a harder nut to
crack in diſcovering the letter of Lorenzo Paſqualigo to his brother (p. 262, ſame volume),
who ſays : " The Venetian, our countryman,
who went with a ſhip from Briſtol in queſt of
new iſlands, is returned, and ſays that 700
leagues hence he diſcovered land, the territory
of the Grand Cham; he coaſted for 300
leagues, and landed; ſaw no human beings,
but he has brought hither to the king certain
ſnares which had been ſet to catch game, and
a needle for making nets ; he alſo found ſome

" Venetian Calendar," p. 262, from " Sanuto Dia- ries," vol. i. p. 573.

felled trees, wherefore he fuppofed there were inhabitants, and returned to his fhip in alarm.

" He was three months on the voyage, and on his return he saw two iflands to ftarboard, but would not land, time being precious, as he was fhort of provifions.

" He fays that the tides are flack, and do not flow as they do here. The King of England is much pleafed with this intelligence.

" The King has promifed that in the fpring our countryman fhall have ten fhips, armed to his order, and at his requeft has conceded him all the prifoners, except fuch as are confined for high treafon, to man his fleet.

" The King has alfo given him money wherewith to amufe himfelf till then, and he is now at Briftol with his wife, who is alfo a Venetian, and with his fons.

" His name is Zuan Cabot, and he is ftyled the Great Admiral; vaft honour is paid him ; he dreffes in filk, and thefe Englifh run after him like mad people, fo that he can enlift as many of them as he pleafes, and a number of our own.

" The difcoverer of thefe places planted on

his new-found lands a large croſs, with one
flag of England and another of St. Mark, by
reaſon of his being a Venetian, ſo that our
banner has floated very far afield.   23rd Auguſt, 1497."

Now the "*amor patria*" is very ſtrong here.
The writer knows John as the head of the
family and as his countryman, and enlarges on
his honours and ſucceſſes.

It ſo happens that we have one little gauge
to teſt the letter by.   In the privy purſe expenſe of Henry VII. Auguſt 10, 1497, is an
entry of the ſum paid: "To him who found
the new iſle, £10,"—a ſum perfectly in keeping with the parſimonious character of the
King, but utterly inſufficient to keep the
"Great Admiral, dreſſed in ſilk, with his wife
and family, till the fleet is ready next year at
Briſtol."

No doubt the wary Venetian would conceal,
as Eraſmus did, the ſmallneſs of the pittance,
and leave it to be inferred that one more com-
menſurate had been received.

If the other particulars of the letter are not
therefore more correct than we have proved

Nicholas'
" Excerpta
Hiſtorica."

Layceys
Eraſmus.

this portion to be, we may yet conceive that

John Cabot
and fons.

John Cabot took no active part in the expedition, and that the acts and deeds of his fon for the *trading firm* are here recorded as the acts of John, the known and refpected head of the faid *firm*.

Sebaftian an
active part-
ner.

At all events, even if John did go, he being at that time, wherever born, a regiftered Venetian citizen, he went for England, and his Briftol born fon and partner failed with him, fharing not only the perfonal rifks, but alfo that of property ; and if John Cabot is entitled to honour, the moiety of it muft equitably belong to his fon Sebaftian.

His portrait
by Holbein,
fee frontif-
piece.

Hanging in the Privy Gallery at Whitehall were once two mute evidences, neither of which can be faid to authoritatively decide this queftion. The firft is a portrait of Sebaftian, by Holbein, with this infcription : " Effigies Seb. Caboti, Angli filii Johan. Caboti, Veneti militis aurati, primi inventoris terræ novæ fub Henrice VII. Anglia Rege."

Purchas'
" Pilgrims,"
vol. iii. p. 807.

The other, the map of Sebaftian Cabot, cut by Clement Adams, concerning his difcovery of the Weft Indies, in which the infcription aſcribed it to the joint agency of both John and Sebaſtian.

The picture, of which we give an engraving, is ſtill in exiſtence in America; " the original map, and the chartes and mappes and diſcourſes, drawn and written by himſelf, were in the cuſtody of the Worſhipful Maſter William Worthington," who was, at the cloſe of Sebaſtian Cabot's life, a ſharer in his penſion and office, and who is ſuppoſed (for a conſideration) to have given them up to Philip of Spain.

Miſſing maps ſuppoſed to have found their way to Spain.

We have already ſeen that in the map of Sebaſtian Cabot, publiſhed in 1544, moſt probably under his immediate ſuperviſion, in Spain, the diſcovery is attributed to both the father and the ſon.

Map in this volume.

The brave and chivalrous Sir Humphrey Gilbert, who was the contemporary of Sebaſtian, ſays, in referring to Cabot's original map, " Furthermore, Sebaſtian Cabot, by his perſonal experience and travel, hath ſet forth and deſcribed this paſſage in his charts, which are yet to be ſeen in the Queen's Majeſty's Privy Gallery at Whitehall, &c. &c."

Sir H. Gilbert on the North-Weſt Paſſage, A. D. 1576.

Portrait of Sebaftian as Worfhipful Governor of the Merchant Adventurers' Company.

Now for the evidence of the portrait: it was painted by Holbein, at a time when Sebaftian was the Worfhipful Governor of the Merchant Adventurers' Company, and, in his official capacity, had under him the Lord High Admiral, the Lord Steward of the Houfehold, the Lord Keeper of the Privy Seal, and the Lord High Treafurer of England, who were his fubordinate affiftants; and all belonged to the company.

He was alfo the higheft naval officer in Spain.

He had alfo for many years held the higheft naval office in Spain; and whilft there is no record of his having been knighted by an Englifh monarch, it is quite poffible that he might have been a knight of Spain or of Venice; one had her knights of the golden fleece, the other her knights of the golden ftole.

Is faid to have been a knight.

More probably John was one of the patrician ar-balaft men appointed to each London galley, the captains of which were alfo always entitled "Ser." See "Venetian Calendar," p. 74.

In one of the ftate papers about 1660, he is referred to as a knight: "Sir Sebaftian Cabot, in the year 1497, employed by Henry VII., &c. &c."

On the other hand, Campbell, in his "Lives of the Admirals," and Dr. Henry, in his "Hiftory of Britain," tell us that John Cabot was knighted, but there is no record of the fact on the rolls.

One ſtrong objection has been made to the knighthood of either of them; and Biddle warmly contends, that if the inſcription meant that the title had been conferred, it would have been Eques, and not Militis.

Biddle's view on this ſubject conſidered. See his "Memoir of Cabot," pp. 182, 325.

That this objection is not valid, any one who viſits the Temple and looks at the Benchers' coats of arms, will be at once convinced; the fact being, that when a member of the bar is knighted the term Miles is uſed to this day; and though Eques is the herald's, Miles is invariably the legal deſignation.

To whom, then, does the latter part of the inſcription belong? We believe to the man whom the picture repreſents; and now let us turn to the account which he is ſaid to have given to a ſtrange gentleman, who, curious in the art of navigation, called on him when he was living in the city of Seville, and years afterwards retailed the information which Sebaſtian Cabot then gave him, to a circle of admiring friends in the villa of the celebrated Italian poet, Fracaſtoro, Ramuſio, the hiſtorian, being preſent; who ſays:—

Cabot's ſtatement to a ſtranger at Seville.

Fracaſtoro the poet.

" It would be inexcuſable in me if I did not

relate a high and admirable difcourfe which, fome *few months ago*, it was my good fortune

" Ramufic," vol. i. fol. 414 D, cd. 1554. See " Plata and Florida."

to hear in company with the excellent architect, Michael de St. Michael, in the fweet and romantic country feat of Hieronymo Fracaftoro, named Caphi, fituated near Verona, whilft we fat on the top of a hill commanding a view of the whole of the Lago di Garda. * * * *

" We found him on our arrival fitting in company with a certain gentleman whofe name, from motives of delicacy and refpect, I conceal. He was, however, a profound philofopher and mathematician. * * * * * At this point, after the ftranger had made a paufe of a few minutes, he turned to us and faid :—

The ftranger's opinion of Seb. Cabot's abilities.

" ' Do you not know, regarding this project of going to India by the north-weft, what was formerly achieved by your fellow-citizen, the Venetian, a moft extraordinary man, and fo deeply converfant in everything connected with navigation and the fcience of cofmography, that in thefe days he hath not his equal in Spain ; infomuch that for his ability he is preferred above all other pilots that fail to the Weft Indies, who may not pafs thither without his

licenſe, on which account he is denominated
Piloto-mayor, or Grand Pilot?"

" When to this queſtion we replied that we
knew him not, the ſtranger proceeded to tell
us that, being ſome years ago in the city of
Seville, he was deſirous to gain an acquaintance
with the navigations of the Spaniards, when he
learnt that there was in the city a valiant man, a
Venetian born, named Sebaſtian Cabot, who had
the charge of thoſe things, being an expert man
in the ſcience of navigation, and one who could
make charts for the ſea with his own hand.

His ſkill in
making
charts.

" Upon this report of him," continued he, " I
ſought his acquaintance and found him a pleaſant and courteous perſon, who loaded me with
kindneſs and ſhowed me many things ; among
the reſt a large map of the world, with the
navigations of the Portugueſe and Spaniards
minutely laid down upon it ; and in exhibiting
this to me he informed me that his father,
many years ago, having left Venice to dwell in
England to follow the trade of merchandiſes,
had taken him to London while he was yet
very young, yet having, neverthelefs, ſome
knowledge of letters, of humanity, and of the

Has a pleaſ-
ing, courteous
manner.

fphere. ' And when my father died,' faid he, 'in that time when news was brought that Don Chriftopher Colonus, Genoefe, had difcovered the coafts of Indies, whereof was great talk in all the court of King Henry VII., who then reigned, infomuch that all men, with great admiration, affirmed it to be a thing more divine than human, to fail by the Weft into the Eaft, where fpices grow, by a way that was never known before; by this fame and report there increafed in my heart a great flame of defire to attempt fome notable thing; and, underftanding by the fphere that, if I fhould fail by way

of the north-weft I fhould, by a fhorter track, come into India, I imparted my ideas to the king, who immediately commanded two caravels to be furnifhed with all things neceffary for the voyage, being much pleafed therewith. This happened in 1496, in the early part of fummer, and I began to fail towards the northweft with the idea that the firft land I fhould make would be Cathay, from which I intended afterwards to direct my courfe to the Indies; but after the lapfe of feveral days, having difcovered it, I found that the coaft ran towards the north, to my great diſappointment. From thence, ſailing along it to aſcertain if I could find any gulf to run into, I could diſcover none; and thus, having proceeded as far as 56° under the pole, and ſeeing that here the coaſt trended towards the Eaſt, I deſpaired of diſcovering any paſſage, and after this turned back to examine the ſame coaſt in its direction towards the equinoctial; always with the ſame object of finding a paſſage to the Indies, and thus at laſt I reached the country at preſent named Florida, where, ſince my proviſions began to fail me, I took the reſolution of returning to England.

Baffled in his ſearch.

Sails towards the equinoctial, and thence home.

" ' On arriving in that country I found great tumults, occaſioned by the riſing of the common people and the war in Scotland; nor was there any more talk of a voyage to theſe parts.

Perkin Warbeck's inſurrection.

" ' For this reaſon I departed into Spain to their moſt Catholic Majeſties, Ferdinand and Iſabella; who having learnt what I had accompliſhed, received me into their ſervice and deſpatched me on a voyage of diſcovery to the coaſt of Brazil, where I found an exceeding deep and mighty river, called at preſent ' La Plata,'

Cabot ſeeks ſervice in Spain.

Explores the
Rio de la
Plata.

Makes many
voyages.

into which I failed and explored its courfe into
the continent more than fix fcore leagues. * * *

" ' After this I made many other voyages,
which I now pretermit, and, growing old, I give
myfelf to reft from fuch labours, becaufe there
are now many young and vigorous feamen of
good experience, by whofe forwardnefs I do
rejoice in the fruit of my labours, and reft with
the charge of this office, as you fee.' "

A thrice-told
tale; fifty
years old
when written
by Ramufio,
who only
gives it as a
general out-
line; hence
not to be li-
terally relied
on.

This vifit muft have been made to Cabot
fome fhort time before his leaving Spain, which
was in 1548; or, in other words, his narration
to the ftranger was between forty and fifty years
after his firft vifit to America, and was evidently
a general refumé of his three voyages to the
north, as well as the one to Brazil.

It was not told to Ramufio until fome years
afterwards, nor does he write it until a lapfe
of months had intervened, and then modeftly
fays that he does not, and cannot, pledge himfelf to accuracy of detail.

" The which difcourfe I have not the courage
to write down as fully as I heard it, for that I
fhould need a capacity and a memory which I
do not poffefs; but I will do my beft, notwith-

ſtanding, to ſketch out briefly, as it were, the heads of what I remember of it."

We could not, for the above and other rea-ſons, expect abſolute accuracy as to the date or the latitudes, but we do certainly gather from the ſimply-told narrative, that Sebaſtian con-ſidered himſelf the diſcoverer, " not thinking to find any other land than that of Cathay."

Whether John Cabot ſailed as Captain-Ge-neral of the expedition, or not, one thing is certain ; Sebaſtian, inſpired with an honourable emulation of the fame of Columbus, was there, we think, as his father's *alter ego*, as well as his partner in the adventure.

Was it then in 1494 or in 1497 that the good ſhip " Matthew," ſailed out of Avon-mouth, Briſtol ? If in only one of theſe years, which was it ? The charters would certainly ſeem to decide in favour of 1497, if it be one only. But we incline to think, for reaſons already given, as well as for thoſe which follow, that it is more than probable that a voyage was made in each of the years above mentioned, and that the firſt diſcovery was really on the 24th of June, 1494 : for if it was on the 24th

The good ſhip " Matthew" ſails from Briſtol.

Reafons in
favour of
there being
two voyages,
one in 1494
and one in
1497.

June, 1497, and the fhip was anything like
the time on her paffage home which fhe took
coming out, there was only three weeks to
explore the three hundred leagues of a ftrange
coaft, in a fea fubjeƈt to fogs, and in which
they would have to guard againft furprifes of
all forts, and literally to feel their way as they
furveyed and examined its rugged fhores,
hitherto untrodden by any European; a feat
that would be impoffible in thefe days of fteam,
much more in a fmall caravel, of the flow-
failing type of that age.

Pafqualigo tells us they were three months
on the voyage; yet we find the head of the
firm, John, at the court in London, and in
poffeffion of the reward on the 10th of Auguft,
1497. The land was feen, it is faid, on June
24th; if they were three months on the
voyage, they failed about the 10th of May,
and were thirty-four days beating out; take
the fame period for their return, including the
landing at Briftol and the two days' journey to
London, and it will juft give three weeks to
do what we venture to fay no hydrographer of
the prefent day, with all the knowledge which

experience has brought, and all the appliances of ſcience, would venture to attempt in leſs than as many months.

Let us try and trace the voyage; the map already referred to ſadly diſarranges all pre-conceived opinions, but gives us the route, and ſome of the anchorages of the expedition.

By it we learn that the adventurers ſailed nearly due weſt; that the firſt land made was the Cape North, the northern extremity of Cape Breton, and the iſland oppoſite the ſame (*not lying in front of the land, but further on*) was Prince Edward's Iſland, which was then named by them and long afterwards known as the Iſle of St. John; that they ſkirted this island, and ſailed along the ſouthern coaſt on the Gulf of St. Lawrence, beyond the ſite on which Quebec at preſent ſtands; that returning by the northern ſhore of the Gulf, " ſtill trending eaſtward," they coaſted to the latitude of 53°, and then, ſailing by Newfoundland Iſland, which they took to be and depict as an archipelago, they continued their courſe ſouthward to the Cheſapeake, and ſo home.

The " Prima Viſta " then was the moſt

Firſt land ſeen, Cape North.

Explores the eſtuary of the St. Lawrence.

Takes New-foundland Iſland to be an archipe-lago.

northerly point of Cape Breton, and the point ſtruck gave them a view at once of Nova Scotia and of Prince Edward's Iſland.

The voyagers in the "Matthew," 1497, ſee no inhabitants.
We muſt here carefully draw the line between this voyage and that deſcribed by Peter Martyr, where the inhabitants, beaſts, and fiſhes were ſeen; that, we ſhall ſhow, was on the next voyage, in 1498, after this exploring one in 1497, for on this it is exprefsly ſtated, by Paſqualigo, that after ſailing on the coaſt for more than 300 leagues, they ſaw no inhabitant, but finding ſome felled trees and a ſnare for game, together with a needle for making nets, they retreated haſtily to their ſhips, and brought the two prizes, the needle and the ſnare, home to England, and ſhewed them to the king, paſſing on their way two

" Venetian Calendar," p. 260.
iſlands to ſtarboard, which the Venetian Envoy deſcribes as being large and fertile new iſlands (does he mean in contradiſtinction to thoſe found in 1494?), but being preſſed for time, and ſhort of proviſions, they haſtened home.

The tides.
They alſo told the king that the tides were ſlack on that coaſt, and did not flow as they do in England.

The intelligent reader will bear in mind that a large portion of the coaſt thus ſurveyed was the ſouthern part of Labrador, and the rugged ſhores of the Gulf of St. Lawrence, which later writers deſcribe as a heap of bare and frightful rocks, a region which even now is, and ever will be, moſt ſparſely populated.

Cartwright's "Sixteen Years in Labrador." "Gazetteer of the World," article "Labrador."

When the voyagers got back into a more genial clime, where they probably ſaw the large and fertile lands, there were two cogent reaſons why they ſhould not land, but at once hurry homewards; had time permitted, doubtleſs they would here have found inhabitants.

Newfoundland Iſland, thought then to be an archipelago.

Sebaſtian Cabot was, as we have ſhewn, in the very prime and vigour of manhood in 1494, being then twenty-two years of age. The above reaſons, combined with the date on the exiſting old map, harmonizing as they do with Cabot's own ſtatement as to the lively emulation cauſed by the diſcoveries of Columbus, ſatisfy us that the firſt land ſeen was Nova Scotia, in the yeaʀ of grace 1494; and that Sebaſtian was one of its diſcoverers, as well as a ſharer in the ſubſequent expedition.

Sebaſtian's age in 1494, when the firſt diſcovery was made.

CHAPTER V.

Was John Cabot knighted? his death. Sebastian in sole command of the expedition under the Charter of 1498. This Charter altogether misunderstood; is a rider on the previous one, allowing colonization, and encouraging trade; annuls no previous privilege; proofs; route now taken by Iceland; lands the emigrants; fails north, enters and partially explores Hudson's Bay, gets among the ice, crew terrified; returns to Baccalaos, describes natives, huge fish, large bears, &c. &c. Corroborative testimony; coasts southward, to Florida and home.

" Venetian Calendar," 12 Ap. 1485.

An admiral for whose board and not his pay he is responsible.

The salary of the admiral paid as usual by the masters, p. 148.

THE Flanders' galleys, which sailed yearly from Venice, calling at England on their way, had a captain general, who was permitted to have an admiral under him; he, the said captain, finding him his board. Whether the elder Cabot was one of these admirals, or sailing masters, is doubtful.

Pasqualigo says the English termed him the

great admiral on his return from his voyage, and then it muſt have been that he was knighted, if ever ; but of this we have ſerious doubts, as there is nothing but the vague inſcription on the portrait to really warrant the ſuppoſition.

Was John Cabot an admiral or ſailing-maſter and pilot, and hence derived a title.

True there ſeems to have been a traditionary rumour to that effeſt, and it is quite poſſible that death may have followed ſo cloſely on the ſpurs of the knight as to leave no trace in hiſtory : for Sebaſtian tells us that about this time his father died, leaving him (Peter Martyr informs us) very rich, and full of ambition.

Ramuſio, " Venice," ed. 1543.

It cannot be ſuppoſed that ſuch a man would lightly abandon that which had been ſo hardly won. He was John Cabot's ſon ; he had at leaſt a fourth ſhare in the patent, had been, if nothing more, a partner in all the previous diſcoveries ; a large ſum had been inveſted by the family, which had brought, as yet, no adequate return ; nothing but an empty title, or right to trade with the new found lands ;—his intereſt, as well as his enthuſiaſm and his ambition, pointed clearly his

adventurous fpirit the road to further exploration and colonization.

The probability is that the fons continued
to trade under the well-known name of their
father, rather than change the title of the
firm.

Ramufio, firft
vol. ed. 1554.
For though it is probable that John Cabot
was alive when the fecond patent was granted,
in February, 1498, it is morally certain that
he was dead when the expedition failed under
the command of Sebaftian.

Much ftrefs has been laid on the fact, that
this fecond patent is made out in the name of
John Cabot only; and the omiffion of the
names of the three fons is thought to be
Biddle's
" Memoirs
of Cabot,"
p. 50.
fomewhat fignificant. The cafe was altered
now, fay they; any feaman could find his way
to the new found land; and the fhrewd avarice
of the penurious king would fee how much
more it was to his intereft to employ profpec-
tive adventurers, rather than thofe whofe
charters would trench heavily on the Royal
prerogative; none could, under the firft charter, trade without a licenfe from the Cabots,
and fo this was made in favour of John, an

aged, ailing, and, as it proved, a dying man: Sebaſtian, by acting under it, waived all perſonal claim under the firſt patent, which, in fact, became a dead letter.

This was entirely of a piece with Henry's general character, who heſitated not to take any advantage, when he had one in his power; witneſs his detention of Philip, king of Caſtile, who, driven by ſtreſs of weather into Portland Roads, was by him detained, on ſpecious pretences, until he had conſented to give his ſiſter to be Queen of England, and to yield up the White Roſe (as Henry's dreaded foe, the Duke of Suffolk, was called by the people) into his hands, to be by him cruelly beheaded.

"Venetian Calendar," Mar. 17, 1506.

A king ſo faithleſs to his peer would not be particular in altering a charter.

But we are not ſo ſure, after all, that the criticiſm is in this caſe a juſt one: after a careful ſtudy of its clauſes, we deem this *charter merely ſupplementary* to that of 1495, giving Cabot extra powers to preſs ſhips at the ſame rate of payment which the king gave for his own ſervice, and to enliſt men for the venture;

The ſecond charter only ſupplementary to that of 1495.

there is in it no bar to his trading or granting licenfes ; no empowering other perfons to trade independently of the Cabot family, and no re- leafe from the one fifth tribute which, under the firft charter, they were to pay to the king out of their profits.

It gives no releafe from the tribute.

Strange to fay, the very exiftence of this patent was unknown until Mr. Biddle, in 1831, by a moft diligent fearch in the Rolls' Office, difcovered, and gave it to the public in his " Memoir of Sebaftian Cabot," a work full of painftaking refearch, and to which we own ourfelves deeply indebted ; though in many points we, with added information fince his day, are conftrained to differ from his conclu- fions.

Biddle's " Cabot," p. 76.

The charter runs thus :—

" Memorandum quod tertio die Februarii Anno Regni Regis Henrici Septimi XIII ifta Bella delibata fuit Domino Cancellario Angliae apud Weftmonafterium exequenda.

" To the Kinge.

" Pleafe it your Highneffe, of your moft noble and haboundant grace, to graunte to

John Kabotto, Venecian your gracious Lettres patents, in due forme, to be made, ac-
cordyng to the tenor hereafter enſuying, and
he ſhall continually pray to God for the pre-
ſervacion of your moſt Noble and Roiall aſ-
tate, long to endure."

" HR   Rex
      " To all men to whom theis Preſenteis
ſhall come ſend Gretyng ; knowe ye that We
of our Grace eſpeciall and for dyvers cauſes
us movying   We have given and graunten
and by theis Preſentis geve and graunte to our
wellbeloved John Kabotto Venecian ſufficiente
Auctorite and power that he by him his De-
putie or Deputies ſufficient may take at his
pleaſure VI Engliſshe ſhippes in any Porte or
Portes or other place within this our realme of
England or obeiſance ſo that and if the ſaid
ſhippes be of the burden of CC tonnes or under
with their apparail requiſite and neceſſarie for
the ſafe conduct of the ſaid ſhippes and them
convey and lede to the *Londe and iſles of late
founde by the ſaid John* in oure name and by
oure commaundement, paying for theym and

*Charter, 3d
Feby., 1498.*

*Himſelf and
deputies, i. e.
his ſons.*

every of theym as and if we ſhould in or for our owen cauſe pay and none otherwiſe.

To receive emigrants.

" And that the ſaid John by hym his De-putie or Deputies ſufficiente maye take and receyve into the ſaid ſhippes and every of them all ſuch maiſters maryners Pages and other ſubjeꞔs as of their owen freewille woll gco and paſſe with him, in the ſame ſhippes to the ſaid *Londe or Iſles* without anye impedy-mente lett. or perturbance of anye of our of-ficers or miniſtres or ſubjeꞔs whatſoever they be by theym to the ſeyd John his Deputie or Deputies and all other our ſaid ſubjeꞔs or anye of theym paſſinge with the ſeyd John in the ſeyd ſhippes to the ſeid Londe or Iſles to be doon or ſuffer to be doon or attempted.

To have the aid of the king's officers.

" Geveng in commandment to all and every our officers miniſters and ſubjeꞔs, ſeying or herying theis our Lettres Patents, withoute anye furthe commandment by us to theyme to be geven, to perfourme and ſocour the ſaide John his Deputie and all our ſeyd ſubjeꞔs ſo paſſynge with him according to the tenor of theis our Lettres Patentis.

" Any ſtatute aꞔe or ordenance to the con-

trarye made or to be made in anywife not-
withftandynge.

" Feby. 3 1498."

Here then we have a fcheme for colonization and trade, as well as for difcovery.

All fubjects who would of their own free
will go were welcome.

Bounties were given to others; in the
Privy Purfe expenfes is a record,—

Bounty given
to emigrants.

" Ap 1 1498. A reward of £2 to Jas
Carter for going to the new Ifle, alfo to Tho'
Bradley, and Launcelot Thirkill, going to the
New Ifle £30. March 22nd. Lancelot has re-
ceived £20 as a preft for his fhippe, going to
New Ilande."

" Excerpta
Hiftorica."

The chronicler here calls it an ifland ; but
the king, who had feen the charts, and heard
the tale of the difcovery, and of the mighty
rivers rufhing into the fea, in his charter calls
it the " Londe and Ifles."

Perkin Warbeck's infurrection had filled
the jails, and the king did not know what to do
with the prifoners ; the Venetian Calendar

" Venetian
Calendar,"
p. 262.

Sanuto's
" Diary,"
Oct. 11,
1497.

tells us, " That the king gave Cabot the fweeping of the prifons, all but thofe guilty of high treafon ;" thefe men could not have been intended as mariners, but were doubtlefs to be fettlers to colonize the land.

Gomara corroborates this, who fays,—" Sebaftian Cabot went alfo to know what manner of lands thefe Indies were to inhabit.

R. Eden's
"Decades,"
fol. 318.

" He had with him 300 men, and directed his courfe by the track of Iceland, upon the Cape of Labrador, at 58 degrees; although he (Cabot) fays much further, affirming that in the month of July there was fuch cold and heaps of ice that he durft pafs no further ; alfo that the days were very long, and in a manner without night, and the nights very clear."

" Certain it is, that at the 60 degrees the longeft day is of eighteen hours."

" But confidering the cold and the ftrangenefs of the unknown land, he turned his courfe from thence to the weft, calling at the Baccalaos for refrefhment, following the coaft to the thirty-eighth degree, from whence he returned to England."

That Cabot took the route of Ifland, i. e.

viâ Iceland, on this voyage, is indeed moſt probable; it lies in the direction in which, he
tells us, he failed. A ſteady and advantageous
commerce had been for years carried on between that iſland and Briſtol.

It is referred to in a quaint old poem called
" The Policy of Keeping the Sea" :—

Hakluyt, vol. i. p. 201.

> " Of Iſland to write is little nede,
> Save of ſtockfiſh ; yet forſooth indeed
> Out of Briſtowe, and coſtes many one,
> Men have practyſed by needle and by ſtone,
> Thitherwards, &c. &c."

We have already ſeen that Henry made a
treaty for freedom of trade with the iſland,
and the idea would ſeem to have been that
Cabot, by thus breaking the voyage, would
leſſen the dread of his timid crew.

Campbell's " Lives of Admirals," vol. i. p. 325.

Purſuing his courſe thence to the weſt, he
ſtruck the coaſt of Labrador (which is named
on his map, " De la Tierra de los Baccalaos"),
Gomara tells us, in latitude fifty-eight degrees,
and here is his deſcription of the land : " Tellus
ſterilis eſt neque ullos fructus affert." " The
foil is abſolutely ſterile, and yieldeth no fruit."
Alſo of the inhabitants, " That they wear
beaſts' ſkins and the inteſtines of animals for

From the in-ſcription on Cabot's map, cut by Clement Adams, ſee Hakluyt, vol. iii. p. 6.

clothing, efteeming them as highly as we do
our precious garments; that their weapons are
the bow and arrow, fpears, darts, flings, and
wooden clubs. That the country is crowded
with ftags of unufual height and fize; alfo with
very large bears, which throw themfelves into
the midft of the fhoals of fifh, and, feizing their
prey, drag them to land and devour them. On
this account they meddle little with men."

Hakluyt, vol. iii.

He further fays they found foles of an ell
long, and fuch abundance of a large fifh called
Baccalaos (cod-fifh) that in fome of the bays
they actually impeded the failing of his fhips;
alfo feals and falmon, in great abundance and
of vaft fize. Hawks, eagles, and other birds
of plumage, akin to the colour of the raven,
were found in great quantities.

Now, thefe things all point to Labrador as
the fpot vifited; the reindeer in herds, the
white bear, or the Efquimaux, feldom or never
vifit Newfoundland, unlefs, perchance, carried
thither on a drifting ice-floe.

The name given to the whole of the lands.

The name by which thefe regions were
fpoken of at home—by which they were defcribed in the charter—was the New-found-

land. Men were not looking for a continent; they only expected to find iſlands ; hence they were ſpoken of as ſuch, and by-and-by the name given to the whole ſettled down on a part, the largeſt iſland, which retains the appellation to this day ; and it is received almoſt as an axiom by the many, that it was the veritable ſpot which was firſt diſcovered by the Briſtol navigator.

Were poetical juſtice rendered to him, however, the whole of the northern continent ſhould be called Cabotia ; for from the 68° N. latitude to the 30°, or from the northernmoſt part of Hudſon's Bay to the Gulf of Mexico, he was the firſt European who ſurveyed its coaſts, or attempted to colonize its deſerted ſhores ; whilſt the ſouthern continent, or at leaſt the weſtern Indies, ſhould bear the honoured name— Columbia.

Reverting now for this voyage to Cabot's ſtatement to Ramuſio's friend, we find him ſtating that he found " the land ſtill continent to the 56° under the pole ; and finding no paſſage, and the land tending eaſtwards, I turned back agayne, and ſailed down by the

Coasts fouth-
ward to
Florida.

coaft of that land toward the equinoctial (ever
with an intent to find the faid paffage to India),
and came to that part of this firm land, which
is now called Florida, where, my victuals failing me, I departed thence, and returned into
England."

This is evidently one of the miftakes of the
narrators as to the latitude reached. He went,
on this third voyage, much further north.

R. Eden,
" Decades,"
&c.&c. 1555.

Peter Martyr, his contemporary, fays " he
went fo far north that it was, in a manner,
continual daylight."

Hakluyt, vol.
iii. p. 26.

Willes fays, " Cabota was not only a fkilful
feaman, but a long traveller, and fuch a one
as entered perfonally that ftrait (leading to
Hudfon's Bay). Sent by King Henry VII.
to make this aforefaid difcovery, as in his own
difcourfe of navigation, you may read in his
chart, drawn with his own hand, that the mouth
of the north-weftern ftrait lieth near the 318
meridian between 61° and 64° N. latitude, in
the elevation containing the fame breadth,
about 10° weft, where it openeth foutherly,
more and more."

This foutherly bend a brave, old Briftol

man, Captain James, explored in 1631, and made a wet dock for his ship of ninety tons by sinking her when the ice set down on the coast, himself and his hardy crew wintering in snow-houses, with tents of sails inside. The following spring they raised their ship, finished surveying James's Bay, and reached home safely.

The strange and dangerous voyages of Capt. James, 1633.

Longitude in those early days was but very imperfectly understood, and was measured from Ferro eastward over the Old World, until it completed its circuit of 360 degrees.

Willes further says in his tract which was expressly written for the use of Sir Martin Frobisher :—

Hakluyt, vol. iii. p. 25.

" Let the gulf be nearer to us than commonly in charts we find it, viz. between 61° and 64° N.L., as Gemma Frisius, in his maps and globes, imagineth it, and so left by *our countryman*, Sebastian Cabot, in his table, which the Earl of Bedford hath at Cheyniès."

Zeigler, in 1532, gives his reasons why it must be a gulf into which Cabot entered, because of the ice ; and Eden says, " Cabot told me the ice was of fresh water."

" Argent," ed. 1532, fol. 92 b.

Thevet, the intimate friend of Cartier, the

" Singularitez de la France Añtarĉïque." Paris, 1558. Chap. 74, fol. 148.

great French navigator of 1534, fays, " It (i.e. Hudfon's Bay) was difcovered by Sebaftian Babate, an *Englifhman*, who perfuaded Henry VII. King of England, that he could go eafily this way by the north to Cathay, and that he would thus obtain fpices and other articles from the Indies, equally as well as the King of Portugal ; added to which, he propofed to eftablifh there a New England, which he did not accomplifh. True it is, he put 300 men on fhore, from the coaft of Iceland, towards the north, where the cold deftroyed nearly the whole company."

Probable fite of the firft colony.

We gather, from the whole, that landing a party, probably about Davis' Inlet or Port Manvers, who were to colonize the country, he failed on, north and by weft, until he reached the above limit. A glance at the map will fhow that this muft have been about the latitude of the Fury, and Hecla Straits, "where the land does trend caft and by north, with an open paffage ;" that here the intenfe cold, combined with the fears of his crew, compelled him to abandon any further progrefs ; for in this extreme north, he fays, he found " monftrous heaps of ice ſwimming on the ſea, and, in a manner, continual daylight," yet ſaw he, " the land in that region free from ice, which had been melted by the heat of the ſun ;" and here alſo we learn from Richard Chancellor, he was placed in imminent danger from a waterſpout.

Eden's
" Gomara,"
fol. 318.

Ibid. fol. 357.

Captain Parry, 350 years afterwards, de-ſcribes the ſame neighbourhood, and at the ſame time of the year (July), as " with very little ſnow upon the ground, and with nume-rous ſtreams of water ruſhing down the hills, and ſparkling in the beams of the morning ſun."

Parry's
" Voyages,"
p. 261.

But there was little to cheer the men in a tranſitory gleam of ſunſhine ; huge bergs towered over their heads, and ſwept about with erratic courſe, threatening to cruſh them ; dark, beetling cliffs protruded their granite peaks above the melting ſnows, whilſt others ſtill ſlumbered, beneath their eternal, unſullied, fleecy coverlid. Huge whales, unſcared by their preſence, toſſed their unwieldly bulk high in the air, making the deep to churn and boil like a pot in their deſcent, or gambolled around, as though miſtaking them for comrades. Mon-

Arctic terrors.

ftroufly large bears, Arctic wolves and foxes, the narwhal or horned whale, and the hideous looking walrus, would probably caufe their terror to culminate.

The firft knowledge of the abfence of darknefs.

The brilliant corufcations of the aurora would deter their advance, and perhaps give them the idea of a world on fire; whilft the mere fact " that there was no night there," a thing never hitherto realized, would naturally exercife a myfterious influence, and create an undefine-able dread in their minds.

It is really not wonderful that they turned and retreated. Coming back to the place where he had left the colonifts, he found them difheartened; perhaps, as Thevet fays, dead,

Thevet's "Singularitez de la France Antarctique," ch. lxxiv. p. 148.

many of them : for even if the fettlement was further fouth, and perchance on the ifland of Newfoundland, a fet of thriftlefs jail-birds would have hard times to fettle down and make themfelves comfortable where nothing could be got but by dint of hard work, and where every Jack was as good as his mafter; away from all control or law. Re-embarking

Eden's "Decades," fol. 318.

the remainder, he failed fouth, paft the fhores of funny Virginia; but no graffy flopes or

verdant plains would tempt the wretched fel-
lows again to land ; fafe on board, they would
truft the treacherous fhore no more : and we
may think it a fpecial Providence that brought
Cabot home from a cruife of over 2000 miles
on the unknown American coaft, with fuch a
crew, and a cargo, confifting mainly of convicts.

Remembering the cuftom of hiring the
mariners by the voyage, it is no wonder that
we are told that they mutinied; and provifions
running fhort when they reached Florida, conftrained him to come home, baffled, but not
conquered.

In "Stow's Annals," 1498, under the
mayoralty of Thomas Purchas, is the following ftatement :

" This year one Sebaftian Gaboto, a Genoa's
fon, born in Briftow, profeffing himfelf to be
expert in knowledge of the circuit of the world,
and iflands of the fame, as by his charts and
other reafonable demonftrations he fhewed,
caufed the King to man and victuall a fhip at
Briftow, to fearch for an ifland which he knew
to be replenifhed with rich commodities. In
the fhip, divers merchants of London adven-

Peter Martyr.

Eden's
" Decades,"
vol. iii. cap.
vi.

Stow's
" Annals."

Hakluyt, vol.
iii. p. 9.

tured ſmall ſtocks; and in the company of this
ſhip failed alſo, out of Briſtow, three or four
ſmall ſhips, fraught with ſleight and groſſe

Briſtol manu-
factures.

wares, as coarſe cloth caps, laces, points, and
ſuch other . . . . of whom in this mayor's time,
came no tidings." That is, they had not returned in October 1498.

Concluſion
arrived at
that Cabot
ſurveyed the
American
coaſt from
Hudſon's Bay
to Florida,
and colonized
it for ſome
months.

From all this, we gather that this voyage
was made for colonization, trade, and diſcovery
combined; that the King ſhared in the expenſe, probably fitting out one ſhip, as well as
helping the men before named ; that the coaſt,
inhabitants, beaſts, fiſh and birds, as well as
Cabot's own map, prove that the ſcene of their
principal operations was the country now known
as Labrador, but then called by Cabot, " The
land of the Baccalaos;" and that Sebaſtian
Cabot was the firſt man who diſcovered Hudſon's Bay, which he afterwards more thoroughly explored in the following reign, in
the year 1517, when he ſpecially failed in the
ſervice of Henry VIII. in ſearch through it of
the North-Weſt Paſſage.

CHAPTER VI.

Services declined by Henry; traditionary ſtatements of intermediate employment. Cabot invited into Spain; Interlude of the four elements; Cabot returns in diſguſt to England; Expedition of Henry VIII. in 1517 A. D., *reaches* 67½° N. L., *further progreſs arreſted by cowardice of Admiral Pert. R. Thorn of Briſtol, his teſtimony; error of Dr. Robertſon.*

N 1499, Cabot proffered his ſervices to Henry VII. for another voyage, but met "with no great or favourable reception from the king." "The fierce and ſtrong wave," ſays Hall, "which devoured the real, and alſo the pretended Earl of Warwick," was gathering and ſwelling all through that year, and the troubled monarch had home cares enough, without any foreign adventures.

Seyer, the Briſtol hiſtorian, ſays that Cabot now, with no extraordinary preparation, ſet forth from Briſtol, and made great diſcoveries.

Seyer's "Hiſtory of Eriſtol."

Hall's "Chronicles," p. 488.

Seyer, vol. ii. p. 208.

Navarette,
vol. iii. p. 41.

Hojeda, a Spanifh navigator, who failed from Spain May 20, 1499, and was abfent one year, found certain Englifhmen at Caqui-baco; and in his account he mentions this, when giving a defcription of the difcoveries of the Englifh under Henry VII.

Ibid. p. 86.
" As that is
the place
where the
Englifh are
known to be
exploring."

Was this Cabot? The probability is great that it was, and that he would take up the thread of the voyage where he dropt it, at Florida, and fo coaft along to the fouthward; this would fpeedily bring him to the fpot where Hojeda found the Englifh.

An idea, founded partly on tradition and from certain payments from the privy purfe, has found fome favour, viz., that he was en-gaged in colonizing Newfoundland, and the neighbourhood. In Nov. 17, 1503, we read:

Privy purfe
expenfes,
Hy. VII.

" To one that brought hawkes from the New-founded ifland, £1."

" 8th April. To a Prieft, that goeth to the new ifland, £2, &c. &c." But we rather in-cline to put thefe to the account of the Portu-guefe and the Briftol merchants, whofe expe-dition failed in 1502; and who were doubtlefs the men who brought over the *Salvages*, who

Rymer, vol.
xiii.

were exhibited before the king in that year. For if, as ſome think, Cabot brought them to England, the novelty would have worn off, and the king have ſeen them, before three years paſſed away.

Beſides, it was ever againſt Cabot's wiſh to lure or ſteal away from their homes the natives of the lands he viſited. It has been ſaid again, that now comes a moſt diſhonourable act on the part of the king. The Cabots had been to great expenſe, and their diſcoveries, though vaſt, had been hitherto unremunerative. Yet, declining Sebaſtian's ſervices in 1499, in 1501 the king granted to certain Portugales, in conjunction with Richard Warde, Thomas Aſhehurſt, and John Thomas, of Briſtol, a charter to trade to theſe lands, which has in it a clauſe, to the effect that they ſhall not be interfered with by any perſons to whom previous grants have been made ; *but in the original roll the pen is drawn through this clauſe,* and the charter is limited to lands before unknown to all Chriſtians; ſo that the king's character is once more redeemed from diſhonour.

Rymer, vol. xiii. p. 42.

Biddle, p. 318.

Lofing fight, for a while, of our great fea-man, let us briefly glance at what his brother navigators have been meanwhile doing.

On Cabot's return from his continental dif-covery, in Auguft, 1497, the news would be at once tranfmitted to Spain, by the ambaffador, who was then in England, negotiating the marriage of Katharine of Arragon with Prince Arthur.

Don Pedro d'Ayola.

Columbus, ftirred with honourable rivalry, urgently preffed for another and immediate expedition; this failing in May, 1498, re-fulted in the difcovery of the continent of South America, by him, fourteen months after the landing of the chartered expedition, under Cabot, in June, 1497, or four years and two months after, Cabot's map fays, the land was by them difcovered.

Navarette, vol. iii. p. 77.

Eight years afterwards, on May 29th, the great Columbus died.

Hojeda, whom we have before mentioned, had with him in his employ, in the year 1499, a Florentine, named Americus Vefputius, on his firft voyage, he having come to Spain to learn navigation, it is more than probable that

Lardner's "Maritime Difcovery."

at Caquibaco, they met the veteran diſcoverer of the continent face to face. Veſputius, at the death of Columbus, became firſt pilot of Spain, and, though never apparently in command of an expedition, ſailed ſeveral times to the newly-found continent, which took its name from him, a mere hireling.

Thus, ſays the Abbé Raynal, "The moment America became known from the reſt of the world, it was diſtinguiſhed by an act of injuſtice." Raynal's "Hiſtory of the Settlement of the Indies."

Veſputius died in 1512; and Ferdinand of Spain, dreading leſt the young King Harry VIII. ſhould pay no reſpect to the Pope's bull, which gave to him the Weſt Indies, was anxious to withdraw from Henry's ſervice, and to attach to his own, the greateſt navigator of the age, now that Columbus was dead. Navarette, vol. iii. p. 305.

With this view, Ferdinand wrote to " Lord Uliby, Captain-General of the King of England, to ſend over Sebaſtian Cabot, he having heard of his ability as a ſeaman." "Cronologico Para. la Hiſtoria." Madrid, 1723; and Herrera, Dec. 1. lib. ix. cap. xiii. " Uliby Spaniſh for Willoughby."

Lord Willoughby was at the head of a commiſſion for raiſing troops in 1511.

On the 13th of September, 1512, Cabot

went to Spain, when the king gave him the title of his captain; retained him in his fervice at a liberal falary, directing him to live at the city of Seville, and there to await his orders.

" Decades,"
lib. ii. cap.
xii.; and lib.
iii. cap. vi.
Peter Martyr fpeaks of him there as " his very friend, whom I ufe familiarly, and delight to have him fometimes keep me company in mine own houfe; for being called out of England, by command of the Catholic King of Caftile, after the death of King Henry VII., he was made *one of our council*, as touching the affair of the New Indies, looking daily for fhips to be furnifhed for him, to difcover this hid fecret of nature, this voyage is appointed to be begun in March, in the year next following, being the year of Chrift 1516." Unfortunately for Cabot, Ferdinand died on the 23rd of January, 1516; and the Spanifh people, being more jealous of foreigners than their late king, the expedition was countermanded, and Cabot, feeling flighted, returned to England, and, under the bluff King Hal, found immediate employment.

The hid fecret
of nature was
this : " Why
the feas in
thefe parts
ran with fo
fwifta current
from the eaft
to the weft."
See p. 231.

It was probably about this time that the
"Interlude of the four Elements," part of
which we give, was written. Dr. Dibdin
dates it A.D. 1510; we think it bears internal
teſtimony of having been ſomewhat later, and
that the Experyens herein depicted was none
other than Sebaſtian Cabot himſelf; if not,
who ſat for the portrait? The age was not
as·yet rich in great Engliſhmen; who were
familiar with not only " certeyne poyntes of
coſmography," but with pretty nearly the
whole circle of natural ſcience; and who, in
deſcribing the ſcenes of foreign travel, and
the ignorance of the natives, could do ſo with
the graphic ſimplicity of enlightened, kind-
hearted eye-witneſſes, who felt that

By Raſtel, brother-in-law to Sir Thomas More.

Hiſtory names no other Engliſhman in whom all this talent and travel meet but Cabot.

> " A greate meritorious dede
> It were to haue the people inſtructede."

An interlude of the four Elements.

" A new interlude and a mery of the nature
of the iiij. elementes declarynge many proper
poyntes of Phyloſophy naturall and of Dyvers
Straunge Landys, and of Dyvers Straunge

Effectys and Caufis; whiche, interlude yf the
hole matter be played wyll conteyne the fpace
of an hour and a halfe but yf ye lyft ye may
leve out muche of the fed mater, as the Mef-
fengers parte, and fome of Natury's parte, and
fome of Experyens parte, and yet the matter
will depend convenyently and then it wyll not
be pafte *thre quarters of an hour of length.*"

Then follows the names of the players, and
the qualities of the Elements; and then—

Figure of the earth,

" Of certayne conclufions provynge that
the yerth muft needs be rounde, and that it
hangyth in the myddes of the fyrmament,
and that it is in cyrcumference above xxj.m.
myle.

and fea.

" Of certeyne conclufions provynge that
the fee lyeth rounde uppon the yerth.

Strange and
new found
lands.

" Of certeyne poyntes of cofmography, as
how and where the fee coveryth the yerth,
and of dyvers ftrange regyons, and landys,
and which wey they lye, and of the newe
founde landys, and the manner of the people.

*   *   *   *   *

Tides.

" Of the caufe of the ebbe and flode of
the fee.

" Of the cauſe of rayne, ſnowe, and hayle.   Meteorology.
" Of the cauſe of wyndys and thondor.
" Of the cauſe of the lyghtnynge, of blaſyng
ſterrys, and flamis fleynge in the ayre.

    *   *   *   *

    *   *   *   * —p. 16.

Studious Deſyre. Na, no dowte yt it is rownde every-
where,
Which I could prove, thou ſhoudeſt not ſay nay,
Yf I had therto any time and leſer ;
But I knowe a man callyd Experyens,   Experyens a
Of dyvers inſtrumentys is never without,   practical
Cowde prove all theſe poyntys, and yet by his ſcyens,   navigator,
Can tell how many myle the erthe is abowte,
And many other ſtraunge concluſions no dowte
His inſtrumentys coulde ſhew the ſo certayn,
That every rude carter ſhold them perſayve playn.
    *   *   *   " —p. 26.

       Enter Experyens.

Stu. Now coſyn Experyens, as I may ſay,
Ye are right welcom to this contrey,
Without any ſayning.
   Exp. Syr, I thanke you therof hertely,
And I am as glad of your company,
As any man lyvynge.
   Stu. Syr I underſtonde that ye have be   who has ſeen
In mauny a ſtraunge countree,   many a
And have had grete felycyté   ſtraunge
Straunge cauſes to ſeke and ſynde.   countree.

Exp. Right farre Syr, I have ridden and gone
And feen ftraunge thinges many a one
In Affryk, Europe, and Ynde ;
Both eft, and weft, I have been farr
North alfo,—and feen the fowth fterr
Bothe by fee and lande,
And ben in fondry nacyons
With peple of dyvers condycyons
Marvelous to underftonde.

Stu. Syr, yf a man have fuch corage
Or devocyon in pylgrymage
Jheruzalem unto
For to accompt the nexte way,
How many myle is it I you pray
From hens theder to goo ?

Exp. Syr, as for alle fuche queftyons
Of townes to know the fytuacyon,
How ferr they be afunder,
And other poyntes of cofmogryfy,
Ye fhall never lerne them more furely
Than by that fygure yonder.
For who that fygure did fyrft devyfe
It feemeth well he was wyfe
And perfect in this fcyens;
For both the fe and lande alfo
Lye trewe, and juft as they fholde do
I know by experyens.

Stu. Who thynk you brought here this fygure ?
Exp. I wot not.
Stu. Certes, Lord Nature,
Hymfelfe not longe agone

In Indies,
eaft and weft,

and can fhow
them on the
globe.

Whiche was here perſonally,
Declarynge hye phyloſophy
And caſte thys fygure purpoſely
For Humanites inſtruccion.
   Exp. Dowtleſſy, right nobly done.
   Stu. Syr, this realme ye know, is callid Englande
Sometyme Brettayne, I underſtonde;
Therefor, I prey you, point with your hande
In what place it ſhulde lye.
   Exp. Syr, this ys Ynglande lyenge here,
And that is Skotlande that joyneth hym nere
Compaſſyd aboute everywhere
With the Occian ſee rownde;
And next from them weſtwardly
Here by hymſelf alone doth lye
Irlande that holſome grounde.
Here than is the narrow ſee
To Calice and Boleyne the next wey
And Flaunders in this parte;
Here lyeth Fraunce next hym joynynge
And Spayne ſouthwarde from thens ſtandynge
And Portyngale in this quart.
This countrey is called Italye
Beholde where Rome in the myddes loth lye,
And Naples here beyonde;
And this lytell ſee that here is
Is callyd the Gulfe of Venys,
And here Venys dothe ſtande.
As for Almayne lyeth this way;
Here lyeth Denmark, and Norway;
And northwarde on thys ſyde

He deſcribes
the countries
of Europe.

Iceland and the Frozen Ocean ;

> *There lyeth Iſelonde where men do fyſhe,*
> *But beyonde that ſo colde it is*
> *No man may there abyde.*
> *This ſee is called the Great Occyan,*
> *So great it is that never man*
> *Coude tell it ſith the world began*

alſo the new lands found within this XX yere;

> *Till now within this XX yere,*
> *Weſtwarde be founde new landes*
> *That we never harde tell of before this*
> *By wrytynge nor other meanys :*
> Yet many nowe have bene there ;
> And that contrey is ſo large of roome.
> Muche lenger then all Criſtendome,
> Without fable or gyle ;
> For dyvers mariners had it tryed

and the coaſt ſide for five thouſand mile ;

> And ſayled ſtreyght by the coſte ſyde
> *Above V thouſande myle !*
> But what commodytes be wythyn
> No man can tell nor well imagin,
> But yet not long ago
> Some men of this contrey went,
> By the kynge's noble conſent,
> It for to ſerche to that extent,
> And coude not be brought therto ;

alſo the reaſon for their return

> But they that were they venteres,
> Have cauſe to curſe their maryners.
> Fals of promys, and diſſemblers
> *That falſely them betrayed,*
> *Which wold take no paine, to ſaile farther*
> *Than their owne lyſt and pleaſure ;*
> *Wherefor that vyage, and dyvers other*

Such kaytyffes have deſtroyed.
O what a thynge had be then
If that they that be Englishmen
Myght have been the furſt of all
That there ſhulde have take poſſeſſyon,
And made furſt buyldynge and habytacion,
A memory perpetuall!
And alſo what an honorable thynge,
Bothe to the realme, and to the Kynge,
To have had his domynyon extendynge
Thereunto ſo farre a grounde,
Which the noble Kynge of late memory,
The moſt wyſe Prince the VIJ. Henry
Cauſed furſt for to be founde,
And what a grete meritoryouſe dede
It were to have the people inſtruſted
To lyve more vertuouſly;
And to lerne to knowe, of men the maner.
And alſo to knowe God theyr maker
Whyche as yet lyve all beſtly;
For they nother knowe God nor the devell,
Nor ever harde telle of hevyn nor hell,
Wrytynge nor other ſcrypture;
But yet in the ſtede of God Almyght,
The honour the ſone for hys grete lyggt,
For that doth them great pleaſure;
Buyldynge nor houſe they have none at all,
But wodes, cotes, and cavys ſmall
No merveyle though it be ſo
For they uſe no maner of yron
Nother in tole nor other wepon

His regret
that coloniza-
tion was thus
fruſtrated.

Henry VII.
died 1509.

Pious wiſhes.

That fhould help them therto ;
Copper they have which is founde
In dyvers places above the grounde,
Yet they dyg not therefor ;
For as I feyd they have no yron,
Wherby they fhuld in the yerth myne,
To ferche for any wore :
Great haboundance of woddes therbe,

Pine forefts.

Moft parte vyr, and pyne apple tree,
Great ryches myght come thereby
Both pyche, and tarre, and fope afshys
As they make in the Eeft landes
By brynnynge thereof only.

Fifh fo plenti-
ful killed with
ftaves.

Fyfhe they have fo great plenté,
That in havyns take and flayne they be
With ftavys withouten fayle.

    Now, Frenchemen and other have founde the trade
That yerely of fyfhe there they lade
Above a C fayle.
But in the fouth part of that contrey
The people there go naked alway
The lande is of fo great hete !
And in the North parte all the clothes
That they were is but beftes fkynnes
They have no nother fete ;
But how the people furft begun
In that contrey or whens they came,
For Clerkes it is a queftyon.
Other things more I have ne ftore
That I coude tel thereof but now no more
Tyll another feafon."

We are, for this next voyage of 1517, largely indebted to Cabot's perfonal friend, Richard Eden, from whom we learn, that " Henry VIII., in the eighth year of his reign, fitted out, furnifhed, and fet forth certain fhips, under the government of Sebaſtian Cabot, yet living (1553), and one Sir Thomas Pert, whofe faint heart was the caufe that voyage took none effect. If" (he continues), " I fay, fuch manly courage had not been wanting, it might happily have come to pafs, that that rich treafurye, called Perularia, which is now in Spain, in the city of Seville, and fo named, (for that in it is kept the infinite riches brought thither from the new found land of Peru), might long fince have been in the Tower of London, to the King's great honour and the wealth of his realm."

Voyage of 1517. Richard Eden's "Munſter," London, ed. 1553.

Pert's cowardice.

All the evidence tends to fhow that the great object of this voyage was to find an opening through Hudfon's Bay to the back of the Newfound land.

The object being to get to India through Hudfon's Bay.

That Chriſtian knight and brave navigator, Sir Humphrey Gilbert, whofe laſt recorded words, as, drifting by his confort fhip, he was feen on the poop, fitting with his book in his hand, were thefe : "Courage, my lads! we are as near heaven at fea as on land," fays "Cabot entered this fame fret, affirming that he failed very far weftward, with a quarter of the north, on the north fide of Labrador, on the 11th of June, until he came to the feptentrional latitude of 67½°, and finding the fea ftill open, might, and would have gone to Cathay, if the mutiny of the mafter and mariners had not been."

Hakluyt, vol. iii. p. 16.

Hiftory of Henry VII.

Lord Bacon relates, "He failed, as he affirmed on his return, and made a chart thereof, very far weftward, with a quarter of the north, on the north fide of Labrador, until he came to the latitude of 67½°, finding the fea ftill open."

Ortelius, "Theatrum Orbis Terrarum."

Ortelius, who tells us he had Cabot's map before him, has drawn one entitled "America five novi orbis defcriptio," in which he depicts the form of Hudfon's Bay, and a channel leading from its northern extremity towards the pole, precifely as it is.

How is it he was fo correct ? Whence did he get his information, but from Cabot ? No

one elſe ever pretended to have been even ſo
far as the opening of the fret or ſtrait, into
the bay ; and could Cabot have drawn it had
he not been there?

Livio Sanuto, a noble Venetian, in his
"Geografia," 1588, makes repeated alluſions to
the map of "Chiariſſimo Sebaſtiano Caboto,"
with whom, through the medium of a friend,
he correſponded, and therein gives a deſcription which minutely correſponds with Sir H.
Gilbert's.

" Geografia,"
1588. Britiſh
Muſeum.

Robert Thorne, another princely Briſtol man,
who died in London in 1532, leaving all his
debtors forgiven, £4440 to charitable objects,
and £5140 to poor relations (immenſe ſums in
thoſe days), in a letter to the King, in 1527,
(adviſing three routes to be taken to get to
Cathay : one by the north-eaſt, afterwards
taken by the unfortunate Willoughby ; one
directly over the pole ; and one to the north-
weſt,) refers to this voyage of Cabot's taken in
that direction.

Stow ſays
Robert
Thorne was
born in 1492.

Hakluyt, vol.
i. p. 212.

" And if they will take their courſe after
they be paſt the pole toward the weſt, they
ſhall go on the back ſide of the New found

land, which of late was difcovered by your
Grace's fubjeƈts (Labrador, and the fouth
coafts of Hudfon's Bay), until they come to
the backfide of the Indies occidental."

Thus, by advancing regularly, by the route
before taken in the north by His Grace's fubjeƈts, the weftern fide of the American continent would be attained ; and further, in fpeak-

Thorn and
Elliott's
voyage.

ing of another effort made under the aufpices
of his own father and Hugh Elliott, both of them
Briftol merchants, who were the fucceffors of
Warde and Thomas in the patent of 1501,
Thorne, alluding to Cabot's voyage, fays:—

Hakluyt, vol.
i. p. 219.

"Of the which there is no doubt, as now
plainly appeareth, if the mariners would then
have been ruled, and followed their pilot's
mind (Cabot), the land of the Weft Indies
(*i.e.* Peru), from whence all the gold cometh,
had been ours."

Well faid Robert Thorn, of Briftol, the
nineteenth century has proved your theory to

Cabot gets
clofe to the
Magnetic
Pole and the
North-Weft
Paffage.

be correƈt ; and Sebaftian Cabot was on the
very verge of the difcovery, having attained to
the ftraits which lead to the magnetic pole,
and within a fhort diftance of the paffage

which McClure, Clintock, and Collinſon have in our time verified.

Cowardice is not an attribute of Britiſh admirals; true, we have had one ſhot, but it is more than queſtionable that he, the victim of political neceſſity, was a coward ; yet amongſt the hoſt of brave old heroes, here is one with a veritable white feather.

Pert ſhows the white feather.

Sir Thomas Pert was a vice-admiral of England ; Richard Eden, in the life-time of Cabot, and in the enjoyment of his friendſhip, makes this grave charge, and actually dedicates his book to the Lord High Admiral of England. Would he have dared to do this if the charge had been falſe ? That it was openly known, and believed to be true, we ſee by Robert Thorne's alluſion to it eleven years afterwards, and alſo that of Sir H. Gilbert. We can find no excuſe. Sir Thomas muſt go down to poſterity as he has come to us, with the brand of coward on his brow.

Duke of Northumberland Lord High Admiral.

Dr. Robertſon, on what we deem moſt fallacious grounds, ſays that now Cabot came home by way of St. Domingo, threatening to attack the Spaniſh dominions there. We be-

Dr. Robertſon's authority is "Oviedo," book xix. cap. xiii. who says an English rover, &c., &c., called at Hispaniola, &c., in MDXXVII. Dr. Robertson has mistaken this date for 1517, confequently it could not be Cabot who was in the Rio de la Plata for Spain in 1527.

Cabot ftudies the variation of the compafs.

lieve that he was too honourable a man; his whole life prefents the picture of an honeft, earneft, forecafting gentleman; who, though not faultlefs, would fcorn to do fo foul an action. Befides, the very next year he was elected to "an high and honourable poft in the Spanifh kingdom," which effectually deftroys this miferable accufation.

Though baffled by poltroonery, and compelled to return to England without accomplifhing his miffion, Cabot did good fervice to fcience by this voyage; the variation of the compafs, and the great dip of the needle, occupied his attention; the inhofpitable fhores of the vaft bay, nearly to its terminal northern point, were mapped and furveyed, and plans for the accurate determination of the longitude alternated with the difficult work of navigating an unknown fea in a high latitude, with a white-livered crew and a craven commander.

But thefe refults were not fatisfactory to the merchants who had adventured their moneys and commodities; and on Cabot's return, the King was full of continental anxieties, whilft London and the whole country was being again ravaged by that awful peſtilence, the ſweating ſicknefs, which fufpended even the ordinary occupations of commerce, and Cabot, who could not be inactive, to whom " labour was reſt," beaten by circumſtances, but not difheartened, finding no opening in England, turned his face to the South-Eaſt.

July to Decr. 1517.

Cabot looks to a South-Eaſt paſſage.

CHAPTER VII.

The Emperor Charles V. appoints Cabot his Pilot-major in
1518 A.D.   Takes him with him from England, to fill
the office in 1520 A.D.   Cabot's interview with Con-
tarini; his duplicity; controversy between Spain and
Portugal respecting the Moluccas; board of geographers;
Cabot their president; decision given in favour of Spain.
Expedition to explore the South-west; Cabot in com-
mand; mutiny; he seizes the ringleaders, puts them
on shore, enters, and explores the Rio de la Plata;
Garcia's false accusation adopted by Southey; explana-
tion; Cabot's justification by the Emperor.

Charles V.
succeeds to
the throne
of Spain.

HARLES V., the talented, youthful monarch of Spain, who had juſt
ſucceeded his grandfather, Ferdinand, now began to enquire what
had become of the expedition of 1516, which
had been planned to explore the Indies; where
was the head that deſigned, and the hand which
drew thoſe wondrous charts of the ſtrange
lands acroſs the ocean?

We can eaſily underſtand how all this originated. Cabot had a friend at court ; An- Anghiera, or Peter Martyr. ghiera, better known as Peter Martyr, was as high in the confidence of Charles, who had juſt given him a rich abbey, as he had been in that of Ferdinand. He died in 1526, and muſt have been now buſy with his great work, " De rebus Oceanicis et orbe Novo Decades ;" and what more natural than that he ſhould deſire to have at his elbow the man who, of all other living, was beſt qualified to give him practical information thereon.

Anghiera was the ſpring that moved the " Herrera," Dec. 3, lib. iii. cap. vii. king ; Cabot was ſought for; in 1518 he was named Pilot-major of Spain, though he did not enter upon the office until Charles viſited England, and took him back with him in 1520. One of the duties was to examine all pilots ; Dec. 2, lib. ix. cap. vii. none of whom could proceed to the Indies without examination and approval by him.

This office was too much of the character of a ſinecure for one of his active habits. That he was on the look out for employment, we Unpubliſhed Diary of Venetian Embaſſy, 1617, by Rawdon Brown. find from his ſtatement to Cardinal Gaſpar Contarini, whom he tells, that he was again offered ſervice under Henry VIII. in 1519, by Cardinal Wolfey, "who told me he would give me high terms if I would fail with an armada of his on a voyage of difcovery; that the veffels were almoft ready, and they had got together 30,000 ducats for their outfit."

(This no doubt explains the delay in his acceptance of the office of Pilot-major, occurring, as it did, between his being nominated in 1518, and his actual entrance on its duties in 1520.)

"I anfwered Wolfey," he continues, "That, being in the fervice of the King of Spain, I could not go without his leave; but, that if free permiffion were conceded to me from hence, I would ferve him."

This expedition of Wolfey's did not ftart till 1527; and on their arrival at St. John's, Newfoundland, they found fourteen fail of Normans, Bretagnes, and Portuguefe there fifhing. Somewhere on their voyage, their pilot and fome of the failors venturing on fhore, were feized, killed, roafted, and eaten in the fight of all on board.

Candour compels us to record here an incident in Cabot's life, which difplays a degree of duplicity which we believe in his latter days he would not have been guilty of.

Cabot's duplicity.

He was leading an indolent life, on a handſome ſalary, but longing for active employment.

Charles V., in 1519, would certainly not conſent to his entering the ſervice of Henry of England, for Henry was at the field of the cloth of gold, aiding Francis of France in his rivalry with Charles for the empire of Germany.

Spain jealous of England,

Such was the jealouſy felt, that though the liſts were ſet up, cloſe to the Spaniſh King's dominions, not a ſingle knight of Spain ſtirred to do honour to theſe pageantries.

From 1520 to 1525, Charles was buſy at war with France; and though he retained the man, he had neither time nor money to ſpare for expeditions of diſcovery.

and at war with France.

Weary with waiting, Cabot ſeems to have turned towards Venice, his father's country, and all but his own.

The Queen of the Adriatic was on the moſt friendly terms with Spain, and might eaſily, if ſhe choſe, get from the Emperor the transfer

Cabot feeks active employ under Venice.

of his fervices. In order to ingratiate himfelf with her ambaffador, he ftrove, therefore, to make himfelf out to be a Venetian, though bred in England : one who was worth a good wage; his prefent mafter was giving him fo much for doing nothing ; he wanted work, but he would not like to take lefs than he was now getting.

This feems to have been the fpirit of the interview: a defire for active and equally remunerative employment; and if the truth ftood in his way, it muft be facrificed in order to gain his end.

Well! " let him that is without fault caft the firft ftone," ever remembering the age in which the event occurred. We give the converfation as Contarini relates it :—

Diaries and Defpatches of Venetian Embafly, 1617-1618, unpublifhed.

" My Lord Ambaffador, to tell you the truth," (juft what people fay when they don't mean to tell it,) " I was born at Venice, but was bred in England, and then entered the fervice of their Catholic Majefties of Spain, and King Ferdinand made me Captain, with a falary of 50,000 maravedis. Subfequently, his prefent Majefty gave me the grade of Pilot-

major, with an additional ſalary of 50,000
maravedis, and 25,000 maravedis beſides, as Ad-
jutant of the Coaſt, forming a total of 125,000
maravedis, or equal to 300 ducats."
Then follows his narration of Wolſey's
offer, after which he goes on to ſay :

"At that period, in converſation one day
with a certain friar, a Venetian, named Sebaftian Colonna, with whom I was on a very
friendly footing, he ſaid to me, ' Maſter Sebaſtian, you take ſuch great pains to benefit
foreigners, and forget your native land : would
it not be poſſible for Venice likewiſe to de-
rive ſome advantage from you ?' "

At this my heart ſmote me, and I told him
I would think about it, and ſo on. On returning to him the next day, I ſaid that I had
the means of rendering Venice a partaker of
this navigation, whereby ſhe would obtain
great profit. " Which is the truth, for I have
diſcovered it."

Contarini compliments him upon his patriotiſm, but doubts the feaſibility of his
ſcheme, and ſtarts difficulties. Cabot contends
that his plan is practicable, and adds :—

He offers to come to Venice at his own charges.

" I will tell you—I would not accept the offer of the King of England, for the fake of benefitting my country." (Alas! poor human nature ; he didn't tell Wolfey fo, but " I will, if the Emperor will let me"). " For if I had liftened to the Englifh propofal, there would have been no more hope for Venice." He then adds : " The way and the means are eafy. I will go to Venice at my own coft ; they fhall hear me, and if they difapprove of the project devifed by me, I will return in' like manner at mine own coft." But he urges Contarini to keep the matter fecret.

But when the Council of Ten fend for him, he declines to leave Spain.

Further communications paffed, and the Council of Ten caufed a letter to be carefully conveyed to Cabot, exhorting him to come to Venice, where he would obtain everything. But meanwhile, other projects arife on the fpot ; active employment is urged on him, and the well-affected patriotifm dies away, or like a garment, is thrown on one fide.

Some one has faid of Cabot, " He was a great liar, as well as a great navigator." We deem this harfh and unfair. A folitary inftance of departure from the truth fhould not ftamp a

man's character; nor was he far from being a
Venetian, whoſe father was one, and who from
four years old to manhood was taught and
trained in that city. Still, it was not the truth;
and whilſt a venial offence, it muſt ever ſtand
as a flaw in his otherwiſe all but unblemiſhed
character.

Nor will the above canting converſation
bear compariſon with his ſimple utterance to
Richard Eden, the friend of his ripeſt years,
the confidant of his voyages, and the ſoother
of his dying hours.

To him he ſays : " I was borne in Bryſtowe,
and at iiij. yeare olde, I was carried with my
father to Venice." He had a golden inducement to lie to Contarini, and he fell under the
temptation. He had no ſuch inducement in
his friendly talk with Eden, and each word
hence bears the ſimple ſtamp of truth.

Rawdon Browne, in a note to the preface to
the " Venetian Calendar," vol. i. p. 78, tells
us that Sebaſtian Cabot took out letters of na-
turalization at Venice, and that the patent is
regiſtered in the book of privileges.

This at once proves that he was not a na-

Cabot's father
a Venetian by
adoption.

His own
ſtatement as
to his birth at
Briſtol.
Eden, Dec.
fol. 255.

" Venetian
Calendar,"
vol. i. p. 78,
ſays Sebaſtian,
by patent,
ecame a
Venetian.

tive. But we rather fufpect that this is a part of the fatality which feems to attend the name, and that this is a miftake, in placing the name Sebaftian for John, for though the two dates 1472 and 1476 are named in the cafe of the father, there is no reference anywhere to the conferring the privilege on the fon, fave in this foot-note.

That North-Weft Paffage was the child of Cabot's earlieft hopes, and though baffled oft, he would, we are certain, be glad to try again. But the cry in Spain was, " To the South ! to the South!" " They that feek riches," faid Peter Martyr, " muft not go to the frozen North."

Spain wanted to get by the fouth-weft to the Moluccas, which fhe claimed. " Not fo," faid Portugal ; " they belong to us, for they are within the limit of longitude covered by the Pope's Bull, which grants all that region to us."

A conference of geographers was therefore fummoned, of which Cabot was the prefident, and young Columbus had alfo a feat at the board.

They met at Badajoz in April 1524, and on the 31ft of May it was decided that the coveted Spice Iſlands were by twenty degrees within the Spaniſh waters.

Portugal retired in diſguſt, and prepared a fleet to enforce its claims, and to deſtroy commerce in thoſe regions.

Portugal ſullen.

Spain, on the contrary, exultant at the deciſion, and eager for the riches of the Eaſt, formed a company, under the higheſt ſanction, and Cabot was ſolicited to take the command ; ſo he gave up Venice.

Spain exultant.

Our merchant prince, Robert Thorne, of Briſtol, then a reſident at Seville, entered into the adventure, principally that two Engliſh friends of his who were ſomewhat learned in coſmography might go in the ſhip, to bring him certain relation of the country, and to acquire expertneſs in the ſcience of navigation. Good Robert deſerved to be rich, for he knew the right way to uſe his wealth. One of theſe friends was George Barlow, of whom more anon.

R. Thorne, of Briſtol, joins the Spaniards in the new adventure.

In September, 1524, Cabot received permiſſion from the Council of the Indies to engage in the enterpriſe, and gave bond to the company for the faithful execution of his truſt.

Cabot receives permiſſion to take the command.

Charles lends them fhips.

The Emperor, on March 4th, 1525, agreed to let them have a fquadron of three veffels of not lefs than 100 tons, and 150 men.

A fmall caravel was added by a private individual (was it Thorne ?), and the title of Captain-General was conferred on Cabot.

His fhare in the antici-pated profit.

The Emperor was to receive 4000 ducats and a fhare of the profits, whilft the whole inveftment of the company only amounted to 10,000 ducats.

Route through Straits of Magellan.

The intention was to fail through the Straits of Magellan, and then thoroughly to explore the weftern fhores of the continent.

Auguft 1525, was the date finally fettled on for failing ; but by fundry intrigues, Portu-

Sail in April 1526.

gal managed to detain the expedition until April 1526.

Not content with foftering difcontent on board the fhips ere they failed, that jealous power continued her machinations at home

Portugal fends a fpying expedition.

and alfo in Spain. She fent out a fquadron, under Garcia, whofe objeĉt was to excite mutiny, to aĉt in concert with the difaffeĉted, and in every way to hinder the progrefs of an expedition commanded by a man who had,

they ſaid, robbed them of the ſpice-bearing
Moluccas.

In April then Cabot ſailed for the Brazils, Cabot's route
by the Canaries, Cape de Verde, and Cape to Brazil.
Auguſtine; though even in this he has been
miſrepreſented by thoſe who wiſhed to detract
from his fame as a navigator.

Petty jealouſy of the great foreigner from
the firſt marred the ſucceſs of the adventure.
The company appointed agents, or deputies,
who were named by the freighters: theſe con- He is croſſed
trolled Cabot in every particular, and were cargos.
conſtantly at croſs purpoſes with him.

He wiſhed to place a man on whom he could
rely (De Rufis) as ſecond in command. The
agents inſiſted on putting Mendez in, as Lieu- Has an ineffi-
tenant-General, whoſe ſole recommendation commander.
ſeems to have been that he had ſailed as purſer
with Magellan.

We may conceive the irkſome poſition of
our countryman, compelled to receive, as his
right hand, a man whom he diſtruſted, and in
reference to whom he had to inſiſt, that, during any unavoidable abſence of his, Mendez
ſhould take no ſtep whatever except he had

orders from himfelf; barring which, he was not to act at all.

He was thus obliged to render his Lieutenant helplefs, in order to reftrain him from mifchief.

Sealed orders given to each fhip, Befides all this, as a crowning folly, fealed orders were given to each fhip, to be opened at fea.

Thefe contained the abfurd provifion, that in cafe of the Captain's death, eleven others fhould fucceed to the command in the rotation in which their names were placed.

If thefe all died, then the furvivors were to caft lots for the Captaincy, &c., &c.

which tend to create difaffection. The refult of this was immediately feen; it really offered a complete premium for murder, and makes Cabot's fafety almoft a fpecial act of Divine Providence.

Difaffection rife, and fown by the red gold of the Portuguefe ere they failed, now broke out to view; thofe higheft in rank, and neareft the prize coveted, were the very worft.

Captain Caro faithful. Out of the whole lot of haughty Dons, the eleventh man, Captain Gregario Caro, Abdiel like, "among the faithlefs faithful only found," was the only one who retained his integrity. The others fancied that they were, each man alone, fit for command; and ſeemed to think that the baton was within their reach.

Scarcely were they out of ſight of land when a report was ſtudiouſly bruited abroad that they were ſhort of proviſions; before they reached the coaſt of Brazil, Mendez was cruſty and inſolent, De Rojas muttered and ſcowled, with fierce beetling brows, and De Rodas ſneered that the Captain was too gentle and mild for ſo arduous a taſk.

Report of ſhortneſs of proviſions.

As they neared the land, the ſtorm mutterings grew louder; and, ſtrutting up and down with their hands on their ſwords, they threatened open violence.

Culminates in a mutiny.

But they completely miſtook their man. The naval heroes of Britain have ever been men, who, gentle as a woman in the calm, could riſe equal to any emergency, and ever preſent an unquailing front to the ſtorm.

Cabot was no longer a mere pilot to a craven, recreant Pert, but an Engliſhman, with a heavy reſponſibility reſting on him, and high in the confidence of his auguſt employer.

Cabot equal to the emergency.

He felt that a bold and daring exercife of rightful authority was now his only chance; and though, as far as we know, he had only two of his own countrymen to back him, amidft a herd of jealous Spaniards, with daunt-

lefs refolution he feized Captain de Rojas, and with an audacious boldnefs that paralyzed the mutineers, took him out of his own fhip and from their very midft, put him, Mendez, and De Rodas, into a boat, and landed them on a fpot where they were compelled to remain until the Portuguefe expedition, under Garcia (which failed in Auguft, four months after Cabot), picked them up, and fent them home in a flave fhip.

The haughty grandees, full of anger at their humiliation, bitterly refented this treatment in a memorial to the Emperor.

Eventually, Cabot fent home George Bar-low and another, whofe reprefentations fo fatif-fied Charles as to the abfolute neceffity of the harfh ftep which had been taken, that he pro-mifed Cabot the needful fuccours, and alfo fent him permiffion to colonize the country.

A conclufive proof of the wifdom of the

courſe adopted is ſeen in this, that, during the
five years that the expedition remained out,
years full of toil, ſuffering, and great privation,
there was no more murmuring, but ever de-
voted fidelity and unity of action.

Yet even our own Southey, in his " Hiſtory of the Brazils," has echoed the calumnies
of Garcia to the diſparagement of Cabot, whom
he accuſes of requiting the goodwill of the
natives, with the uſual villainy of an old ex-
plorer, by carrying away four of them; and
he alſo denounces as an act of cruelty the ſtep
by which he quelled the mutiny, and, without
Bloodſhed, ſaved the lives of probably many
others beſides his own.

Southey's
adoption from
Garcia of the
calumnies
againſt Cabot.

Let us briefly examine theſe accuſations;
and, firſt, who is the accuſer: Diego Garcia,
a Portugueſe, who ſailed four months after
Cabot, whoſe object was to injure and prevent
the ſucceſs of Cabot's expedition; he had a ſhip
of 100 tons, a pinnace, one brigantine, and the
frame of another, ready to be put together at
need.

The object of
the accuſer.

Touching at the Bay of St. Vincent, Garcia
found a Portugueſe, of the degree of a Bache-

Garcia's
voyage.

lor, whofe fon-in-law accompanied him to the La Plata.

Garcia difpofes of his largeft fhip to be ufed as a flaver,

Finding, on reaching that river, a garrifon of Cabot's, and learning that he, with his fhips, had gone up the ftream, he followed with his brigantine; he had previoufly hired to his hoft at St. Vincent the fhip of 100 tons to carry flaves, and between them they fhipped and fent home 800 natives.

This he did on the abfurd pretence of its being too large for exploring purpofes.

for his own profit.

Yet this man, a fharer in the nefarious trade to fuch an extent, convicted of defrauding his employers, and, by his covetoufnefs, nullifying the object of his own expedition, is the only accufer of Cabot, who, he fays, took from an ifland in the river four fons of chiefs.

Before we take the word of a tainted witnefs, fuch as this man, let us look at the reported facts.

The place and the afferted time of the abduction of natives by Cabot.

It was at the ifland of St. Catharine's, on the coaft of Brazil, on his outward voyage, when, if taken, thefe men would be for years of not the flighteft ufe, but only fo many more mouths to fill. It was not from an ifland in the river, ſo that it could not be in order to uſe them as pilots.

Was nearly 500 miles north of the Rio de la Plata.

Neither, as yet, had Cabot determined to go into the river at all; his doing ſo was only the reſult of the mutiny. If the expedition had been on its return the men would have been worth ſomething, perchance, in Spain. But Cabot was a prominent member of the Council of the Indies, in Spain, was familiar with, and had been inſtrumental in framing their orders, which were peremptory as to offering violence to the Indians.

Cabot's own law againſt violence to the Indians.

When Gomez returned from his voyage, having abducted and brought home ſome of the natives, Cabot was at Seville, and knew well the cry of indignation that rang through the land.

Gomez's voyage, 1524.

In after life, in his own inſtructions to Willoughby, he enjoins every effort, by gentleneſs, to get a thorough knowledge of the natives, and he expreſsly forbids the uſe of violence or force.

Hakluyt, vol. i. p. 228.

Beſides, Garcia called at the iſland, a ſtrange European, when the wound, if there was one, was raw, and admits that he was gracioufly re-

ceived! Is it credible? Would they not rather
have confounded him with the others, who had
committed the outrage and wreaked their vengeance on him?

There is only one plaufible theory, one
which we have never yet feen broached, and yet
it forcibly croffes our minds in looking at this
fubject. If he did take thefe chiefs' fons, was
it as hoftages for the good treatment of the
mutineers, whom he landed fomewhere about
here, very probably on this ifland, intending
to pick them up on his return voyage?

If fo, Garcia's reception proves that the exchange was a voluntary one, and the charge
of treachery difappears; and he who took fuch
meafures to preferve the lives of the men
who endeavoured to fubvert all authority can
furely not be called cruel.

The ejection from the fleet of the mutineers
was the mildeft as well as the fafeft thing that
could be done, and, we fee, was executed with
as much mildnefs as was confiftent with a fenfe
of duty.

It is a remarkable fact, that if there is one
perfonal trait in Sebaftian Cabot's life more

prominent than another, it is his gentleneſs. All who enjoyed perſonal intercourſe, or were brought into cloſe connection with him, ſeem to have loved him ; and ever and anon they break out into expreſſions of affectionate attachment.

To a phyſiognomiſt his portrait will at once exonerate him from ſuch a charge ; there is no cruelty written on that brow, or gleaming from thoſe mild eyes.

We diſmiſs theſe calumnies, therefore, with one remark.

On Cabot's return to Spain the Emperor, who had meanwhile ſuperſeded the company, and taken all the expenſes on himſelf, rein-ſtated him at once in his high and honourable office ; and when, afterwards, Cabot went to England, made inceſſant and moſt importunate interceſſions, through his ambaſſador, to get him to return and ſettle in Spain. This com-pletes, we think, his vindication.

CHAPTER VIII.

*Continues his refearches on the La Plata; builds forts;
afcends the Paraguay; conquers the attacking Guarani
Indians; Garcia's arrival; its confequences; Cabot
wins the love of the natives; cultivates the foil; ftudies
the natural hiftory of the country; makes laws; ad-
minifters juftice; confolidates his power. Treachery of
Garcia's men; natives carry Fort San Spiritus and
deftroy them and that portion of Cabot's men who were
there. Endeavour of the Indians to furprife Cabot;
he beats them off. Embarks for Spain; refumes his
high poft and its emoluments for eighteen years. Returns to his native place, Briftol, and fettles there; probable reafons why. Spanifh Ambaffador demands his
return of King Edward and his council; Cabot's interview and reply. Spain ftrikes off his penfion; King
Edward grants him one.*

HOUGH Cabot, by his firmnefs,
had diffipated the mutiny, he did
not feel himfelf juftified in profecu-
ting the long and perilous voyage
originally contemplated without confulting his
auguft employer; he therefore put into the

Cabot puts
into the Rio
de la Plata.

Rio de la Plata, and from thence ſent home Hernando Calderon and George Barlow with a ſtatement of all that had occurred.

Sends home Barlow and Calderon, to counteraĉt the ſtate- ments of the mutineers.

The expelled commanders were men of high rank, and great influence at home.

Miguel de Rodas had been with Magellan in his ſhip the " Viĉtory," which circumnavigated the globe. The Emperor had given him a penſion for life and a device for his coat-of-arms, commemorative of that achievement.

Martin Mendez had been in the ſame ſhip, and the device prepared for him was of a yet more flattering deſcription.

Probably their accidental aſſociation with ſo great an enterpriſe had given them a reputation far beyond their deſert; at all events, they were men whom Cabot could not afford to deſpiſe.

Meanwhile our intrepid navigator had loſt no time. His immediate predeceſſor as Pilot-major, De Solis, had diſcovered this vaſt river, whoſe mouth is an inlet of 150 miles in width, and on an iſland in it had loſt his life.

The Plata previouſly diſcovered by De Solis. Gomara, cap. 89.

Cabot puſhed his way up to this ſpot, and

"Decades,"
iii.
Herrera,
lib. ix. cap. iii.

finding a vaſt body of water ſtill deſcending, and precious metals more abundant among the natives the higher he went, he, hoping to be able to ſend home a favourable report, proſecuted his reſearches before he ſent home his meſſengers.

One of his three ſhips had been loſt on the voyage, and the men, who ſaved themſelves by ſwimming, were now diſtributed between the two ſhips and the caravel.

R. Eden's
"Decades,"
fol. 316.

Puſhing his way then boldly up this broad but ſhallow inlet, whoſe intricate navigation and violent pamperos make it to this hour the dread of the navigator, he reached an iſland, which ſtill bears the name he gave to it, St. Gabriel.

The low ſhelving ſhores on either hand gave ſuch ſhallow water that he cared not to take his ſhips near the mainland.

" Iſle of
Martin
Garcia," the
ſcene of the
death of
De Solis.
Gomara,
cap. lxxxix.

Near St. Gabriel was another iſland, where poor De Solis lay buried. He had reached thus far when, in an unfortunate diſpute with the natives, he was ſet upon, killed, together with fifty of his men, and eaten ; though how they managed to eat him and alſo to bury him is a problem which our informant, Herrera, has left unſolved.

Here the natives aſſembled in numbers, and made a great ſhow of reſiſtance, but Eden ſays, "Cabot, without reſpect of peril, thought beſt to expugne it by one means or other, wherein his boldneſs tooke goode effecte, as often tymes chaunceth in grate affayres."

R. Eden's "Decades," fol. 316.

At St. Gabriel he left his ſhips, and in his boats explored ſeven leagues up the ſtream, until he reached another river, to a port cloſe to the mouth of which he gave the name of St. Salvador; and, as it offered a good harbour, he returned and brought thither his ſhips, having, however, to lighten them ere he could get them in.

Hakluyt, vol. iii. p. 729.

This would ſeem to have been on the Rio Naranjos, or the lower branch of the mouth of the Parana, near its confluence with the Uruguay.

Herrera, Dec. iv. lib. viii. cap. ix.

Here, in an iſland about two leagues from the ſpot where De Solis periſhed, he erected a fort, which was ſtanding in 1586.

Though the Uruguay was a very large river, he avoided it, for the ſame reaſon that

Avoids the River Uruguay,

his object being to get westwards.

led him afterwards to pass the mouth of the noble Parana—he saw thefe both led from the North, and his great object was to get, not into Brazil, but to the Weft, becaufe he found that it was from thence the filver came of which the natives were poffeffed.

Two of his men killed.

During the building of this fort the firft blood was fhed. The natives killed and carried off two of the Spaniards, but, in fierce derifion, faid they would not eat them, becaufe they were foldiers, of whofe flefh they had already had a furfeit in De Solis and his followers.

Antonio de Grajeda left in command of the fort.

In this port Cabot left his fhips and a garrifon under the command of Antonio de Grajeda, having firft cut down the caravel for the convenience of river navigation ; and with her and the boats he now proceeded up the Parana.

Builds another fort at Terceiro.

On arriving at the junction of the Carcarama, or Terceiro, he built near it a fort, finding, as he faid, that the natives were intelligent.

Gives the command of it to Gregorio Caro.

This he garrifoned with a party under the command of the faithful Gregorio Caro, the captain of the Maria del Efpinar.

Having thus carefully fecured a bafe in cafe His prudence. of having to retreat, he, with his greatly-weakened troop, puſhed boldly, but carefully, up the river.

Reaching the Parana's junction with the Leaves the larger river and ſtill puſhes weſt-wards. Paraguay, though in reality the largeſt of the two ſtreams, he left it on the right hand, be-caufe the direction whence it flowed was not the route he was anxious to take, and for thirty-four leagues farther urged his way up the Paraguay.

Defcribing this voyage in the converfation Rich. Eden's " Decades," fol. 255. with Ramufio's friend, he fays, "I found an exceedingly large and great river, named at this prefent time the Rio de la Plata—that is, the river of filver—into which I failed, and followed it into the firme land more than 120 leagues, finding it everywhere very faire, and inhabited with infinite people, which, with Ramufio, tom. i. fol. 415. admiration, came running daily to our ſhips. Into this river run fo many other rivers that it is in manner incredible."

The region which our traveller had now reached prefented an entirely new afpect, being everywhere cultivated; and the feeling which

The natives a fuperior clafs, who cultivate the foil. naturally fprings from exclufive poffeffion of the foil led the natives to look with great jealoufy on the intruders, which ripened eventually into the fierceft and moft deadly animofity.

Spaniards feized. Three of the Spaniards, having ftrayed to gather the fruit of the palm-tree, were feized by the natives.

Great battle; Cabot victorious, but with heavy lofs. Herrera, Dec. iv. lib. i. cap. i. Cabot rufhed to the refcue, and a moft fanguinary battle enfued; three hundred of the natives fell, but his fmall party loft twenty-five of their number—a moft ferious lofs, which fo reduced their ftrength as to make further progrefs impracticable.

He apprifes Caro by letter. Like a wife commander, he at once fent down his wounded, and apprifed the garrifon below of his lofs and their danger.

Garcia arrives in the river. Herrera, Dec. iv. lib. i. cap. i. Juft then Garcia had arrived at St. Salvador, and Grajeda, who was in command, thinking that it was the mutineers, manned his boats and proceeded in force againft him. Garcia made himfelf known, and the two parties entered the port amicably.

From hence Garcia fent his fhip to fulfil the contract he had made for carrying the ſlaves, who were natives ſtolen from the Brazil coaſt.

With ſixty men in his two brigantines he aſcended the river to fort Santus Spiritus; here he ſummoned Caro to give him immediate poſſeſſion in the name of the Emperor, contending that he had orders which gave him the rights of diſcovery, though he was ſix months later on the ground than Cabot. Garcia's ſummons to Caro.

Caro told him that he held the fort in the name of the Emperor and Sebaſtian Cabot, but was quite willing to give him a welcome, and all the aid he needed, though he would never ſurrender it. Caro's noble anſwer;

However, he begged Garcia, as a perſonal favour, to look out for wounded Spaniards, or any who were priſoners, and ſaid that he himſelf would repay him if he found any on his aſcent of the river, for, though Cabot had defeated the Indians, there might, he thought it poſſible, be ſome of their people in their hands. But Garcia, inſtead of at once proceeding to the relief of his fellow Europeans on reaching the Parana, ſailed up it for ſome diſtance; nor do we hear of him at Santa Ana and his offer of perſonal indemnity for loſs. Garcia's heartleſs conduct.

until Cabot had come to a good underſtanding with the natives, and all was proſperity and peace.

Cabot and Garcia meet.

Of the interview between the two commanders we know nothing but the reſult.

It was not confiſtent with Cabot's known character, and his high ſtanding in Spain, to ſtruggle for lawleſs or even for doubtful power.

Cabot's characteriſtic deciſion.

His commiſſion did not directly cover his preſent operations, though it might do ſo indirectly; ſo he deſcended the river with Garcia to Salvador, and thence ſent home Barlow and Calderon, as we have ſhown, with a comprehenſive ſtatement of all the incidents which had occurred ſince he left Seville, and the circumſtances which had led him to alter his courſe.

Charles the Fifth's deciſion.

The Emperor heard Barlow and Calderon as well as the mutineers, whom he cauſed to be ſent for, and evidently arrived at the concluſion, that the latter were rightly ſerved; for he ſent word to Cabot that he was to colonize the country, and promiſed ſpeedily to furniſh him with the neceſſary means.

Cabot, with his expectations raiſed to the

higheſt pitch, was moſt eager to carry on the enterprife.

He had reached the waters, which, rifing in Potofi, fall into the Paraguay, and had diſcovered the ſource from which the natives obtained the precious metal which was freely in ufe amongſt them.

The obſtacles between Fort Ana and Peru were trifling; he was all but within reach of the Golden Empire which Pizarro a few years later, by another route, feized on. He had already beaten, and then negotiated a peace, with the fierce Guaranis, who had invaded Peru; and, by friendly intercourfe, had attached them to himfelf, learned many fecrets of that country, and procured from them much gold and filver, which they had brought from thence.

Surely if, with a mere handful of men, he had beaten and conquered the fierce people who had overrun and defpoiled fo rich a region, with a few more foldiers, he might enter and take poffeffion of New Caſtile, the Golden.

But, Tantalus-like, the cup was again to be daſhed from his mouth.

Cabot's furtheſt inland point within fight of the mountains of Peru.

Had beaten the Indians, who had conquered Peru, with an abfurdly fmall force, but was to be difappointed.

The Emperor poor.

Charles V. had outrun his exchequer, and was afflicted with a difeafe very prevalent, in modern days, impecuniofity. His cortes refufed him money. He had mortgaged the Moluccas to Portugal, and his treafury was empty.

Pizarro importunate and fpecious,

Juft then Pizarro, overflowing with ambition, well known at court, perfonally importunate, but afking for no money, only for the government of the countries which he might conquer, affailed the Emperor continually.

and Cabot is neglected.

Cabot was fhelved, Pizarro fucceeded ; of his fuccefsful but infamous career we need fay no more than this, that if Cabot had achieved the conqueft of Peru the blackeft page in the hiftory of Spanifh America would never have been written.

Waiting, he works, raifes crops, experiments on the foil.

Whilft waiting, fick at heart, with hope deferred, Cabot erected forts, adminiftered juftice, and reduced all the furrounding nations to obedience to the Emperor. Ever active, when no fupplies came from Spain, he fet the whole party to work, rapidly raifed fufficient food, made experiments on the fertility of the foil, carefully noting the

reſults, which, with great minuteneſs, he afterwards reported to the Emperor.

He claſſified alſo the various productions
of the country, and graphically deſcribes the
marvellous fecundity of the ſwine, and alſo of
the horſes, both of which they had imported
from Spain; theſe latter became the parent
ſtock whence ſprung the vaſt wild hordes
which ſcour the Pampas to this day.

Claſſifies pro-
ductions, and
points out the
favourable
ſituations for
rearing and
breeding
cattle.

A clever wit of the laſt generation ſaid of
a certain nobleman, that he was ready to take
the helm of the ſtate, or the command of the
channel fleet, at an hour's notice. It was
witty, but not new; for here we actually have
the greateſt commander and navigator of his
age, organizing a nation from the moſt diſ-
cordant elements, and developing its powers
under manifeſt diſadvantages.

We are naturally proud of the Briſtol
mariner, whoſe perſonal agency gave to England and her ſturdy offspring their vaſt poſſeſſions in the north, and to Spain the rich
and well watered regions in the ſouth, of the
American continent; and if any one ſhould
be at all curious to ſee his monument in his

Briſtol proud
of the man
that gave to
England and
to America
and Spain
their vaſt
poſſeſſions.

But rears him no monument. native city, let them know that it lies with Sir Thomas Lawrence's, in the vaft limbo of futurity.

Is five years in the Plata. In the midft of his labours, and, remember, they extended over five years in this region, the fame evil genius which had followed him acrofs the Atlantic was conftantly marring his efforts, and finally ftruck a well-nigh fatal blow to the expedition.

Garcia leaves fome of his fpies behind, Garcia had fwept the country and failed with his fpoil; but he had left behind him a party of his followers, who held themfelves amenable to no law.

who anger the natives. Thefe men, located at Santus Spiritus, were guilty of fome acts of atrocity towards the natives, which roufed their wildeft refentment.

It is exprefsly ftated that with this act, whatever it was, Cabot had nothing at all to do; but the fierce and fanguinary Indians made no diftinction.

Thefe decide on exterminating the whites. Secret meetings were held, a plan of action was decided upon, and it was determined to cut off every white man in the country.

A little before daybreak the enraged nation burft, with one fell fwoop, down on and carried the entrenchments of Santus Spiritus, put-ting the feeble garriſon to the ſword.

They attack
Santus Spiri-
tus, ſlay Caro
and his gar-
riſon.

Here Caro, the faithful, probably periſhed in command, for we henceforth loſe ſight of him.

Maddened with ſucceſs, they rapidly tra-verſe the intervening country, and try the ſame tactics at Fort Salvador.

Swoop down
on Fort Sal-
vador.

But better watch and ward is kept here. " Defence, not Defiance," is the Briſtol man's motto, or rather, as on his portrait, " Spes mea in Deo eſt;" but he watches, as well as hopes; fights, as well as prays; and beats the enemy off.

Cabot on the
watch, beats
them off;

Sad faces come down the river a few days afterwards, re-inforcements, ſent to alarm and put the advance garriſon on their guard, return diſpirited : they had found Santus Spiritus deſolate, a ruin ; and their friends and com-panions ſlain to a man. So Cabot ſhips the requiſite ſupplies, diſmantles the fort, embarks the remnant of his people, and quits for ever the ill-omened ſhore.

and for want
of re-inforce-
ments returns
to Spain.

Herrera, Dec.
iv. lib. viii.
cap. ix.

Five and thirty years, replete with toil, anxiety, and peril, have paſſed away ſince the

Cabot re-
fumes office
in Spain,
A.D. 1531.

date of the firft patent of Henry VII. ; and though Cabot, on his return to Spain, refumes his high ftation, and might bafk at leifure in the emoluments of office, yet we find his fpirit and love of enterprife unbroken, drawing him we know not whither, but repeatedly to fea ; for he fays:

Ramufio,
tom.i.fol.414,
D. Eden, or
1554.

" After this, I made many other voyages, which I now pretermit ; and, growing old, I give myfelf to reft from fuch labours, becaufe there are now many young and vigorous fea-men of good experience, by whofe forwardnefs I do rejoice in the fruit of my labours, and reft with the charge of this office, as you fee."

Some hope
that under
the new re-
gime Spain
may find the
record of
Cabot's
voyages.

So great a change has of late come over the kingdom of Spain, that we may now indulge a hope that the archives of that ancient king-dom will be opened to the ftudent, and that from its hidden treafures fome records of thefe loft voyages, and perchance the invaluable maps and charts drawn by Cabot's own hand, be brought to light ; we indicate a rich mine, who will go and dig ?

Home ficknefs affects, more or lefs, all men at fome period or other of their fojourn in a foreign clime; we have known men, who, under the ſunny, cloudleſs azure of a Naples ſky, ſighed and ſickened for the miſty cloudineſs of our native iſle.

It might have been this that brought Cabot home to Briſtol, no diſhonourable ſlight had been put upon him; for eighteen years he had moved amongſt the grandees of Spain as their equal, and was above the reach of want; we look, at firſt, for any other cauſe, it lies not on the ſurface, perhaps, with induſtry, we may ſtrike the vein.

Cabot returns home.

Barrow, indeed, ſays that "his friend, Robert Thorne, ſent for him home;" verily, if it were ſo, the meſſage was a long time travelling to him, for good Robert Thorne had reſted from his labours for ſixteen years, leaving his works to follow him, as they do this day, and a memory green and beautiful for ever.

Barrow's miſtake as to the cauſe of his return. "Ch. Hiſt. of Voyages," p. 36.

Now Strype tells us that he came to England and ſettled in his native place, Briſtol, in 1548; that is, in the firſt year of Edward VI., and the time of liberty for tender conſciences.

"Hiſtorical Memoirs," vol. ii. p. 190.

Had he, with his gentle and travel-enlarged

heart, who had feen fo much of iniquity practifed in the name of religion by the Spaniards,
conceived a defire in the autumn of his days
to learn fomething of this new religion which
the priefts, who had fanctioned the cruelties of
Mexico and Peru, were everywhere fpeaking
againft; and did he defire liberty for himfelf
to read the Word of God, which he could not
do in Spain? That he was well acquainted
with the letter, and thoroughly entered into
its fublime precepts, we fhall fhortly fee:
fomewhere he learned to reftrain that unruly
member which, once at leaft, led him aftray;
and, not only could he denounce blafphemy
of God, and deteftable fwearing, then fo common, but alfo "ribaldrie, filthy tales, diceing,
and gaming." He alfo is found advifing
morning and evening prayers daily; and alfo
that "the Bible be daily read devoutly and
Chriftianly to God's honour, and for His
grace to be obtained by humble and hearty
prayer."

Here we have, we think, the key to the
myftery, and can underftand why he aban-
doned the emoluments and honours of office,

Theory that it was to enjey liberty of confcience that he returned, a lover of truth and a denouncer of the common vices of all ranks, but efpecially thofe practifed by the feamen of thofe days.

A reader of the Bible and a lover of prayer.

and fteadily and perfiftently refufed to return, but chofe to live and die in a land where, at that time, liberty of confcience was allowed to all men.

Home to Briftol then he came ; but not long had fettled down when a formal and moft urgent demand was made by the Spanifh ambaffador, that

Settled at Briftol, the Spanifh Ambaffador demands his return from the Council.

" Sebaftian Cabote, Grand Pilot of the Emperor's Indies, then in England, might be fent over to Spain, as a very neceffary man for the Emperor, whofe fervant he was, and who had given him a penfion."

Strype, " Hift. Mem." vol.ii. p. 190.

The anfwer to this application is ftill preferved amongft the Harleian MSS., and it goes very far to prove that there had been no quarrel between the Emperor and Cabot.

No. 523, Art. 2, "Letter to Sir Philip Hoby."

The Englifh Council, in its own anxiety to retain Cabot in this country, does fcant juftice to his dignified and fitting reply when pointedly and rudely interrogated as to what he would do at the command of the council or of his fovereign.

This is the narrative of the occurrence: " And as for Sebaftian Cabot, word was firft made that he was not detain'd here by us, but that he of himfelf refufed to go either into Spain or to the Emperor in Flanders; and that he being of that mind, and the King Edward's fubject (Briftol born), no reafon or equity would that he fhould be forced or compelled to go againft his will.

" Upon the which anfwer the ambaffador demanded that Cabot fhould vivâ voce, in the prefence of fome one whom the council fhould appoint, declare this to be his mind and anfwer.

At which
Cabot de-
cidedly re-
fufes to go
either into
Spain or
Flanders,

" Whereunto we condefcended, and at the laft fent the faid Cabot, with Richard Shelley, to the ambaffador, who, as the faid Shelley hath made report to us, affirmed to the faid ambaffador that he was not minded to go, neither into Spain nor to the Emperor.

but is willing
to give the
Emperor all
the informa-
tion he feeks.

" Neverthelefs, having knowledge of certain things very neceffary for the Emperor's knowledge, he was well contented, *for the good-will he bore the Emperor,* to write his mind unto him, or to declare the fame here to any fuch as fhould be appointed to hear him.

" Whereunto the faid ambaffador afked the

faid Cabot, 'in cafe the King's majeſty, or we the council, ſhould command him to go, whether then he would not do it.'"

"Whereunto the faid Cabot made anſwer: '*If* the King's Highneſs, or *we*, ſhould ſo command, he knew well enough what he had to do.'" "But it ſeemeth that the ambaſſador took this anſwer of Cabot to mean that, on being ſo commanded by the King or by us, he would be content to go."

Cabot anſwers the ambaſſador.

"Wherein we reckon the ſaid ambaſſador to be deceived, for Cabot had divers times before declared unto us that he was fully determined not to go hence at all."

Tells the Council he certainly will not go.

Spain, of courſe, ſtruck off his penſion, and Edward immediately gave him one of 250 marks, or £166 13s. 4d., a very handſome ſum for the period.

Spain ſtops his penſion, Edward gives him one.

CHAPTER IX.

Cabot's office; he explains the variation of the Compass to the King; State of Trade in England; depression thereof, caused by the monopoly of the Stilliard merchants. The London merchants consult Cabot; his advice followed; is made Governor of the Merchant Adventurers' Company for life; frequent interviews with the King; breaks the foreign monopoly; is liberally rewarded by the grateful monarch; builds the ships for the new expedition at Bristol, sheaths them with lead plates; first introduction of this system into England; Sir Hugh Willoughby chosen for the command; Cabot's wise sailing and business instructions.

Cabot is made superintendent of the naval affairs of the kingdom.

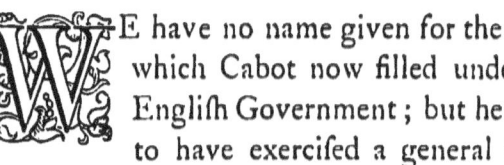E have no name given for the office which Cabot now filled under the English Government; but he seems to have exercised a general supervision over the maritime affairs of the kingdom, under the king and the council. We have one instance left on record in which he vetoed John Allday, who, " Wanting to go as master in a ship to the Levant, was stayed

'By the prince's letters, which my maſter, He licenſes, Sebaſtian Gabote, had obtained for that purpoſe, to my great grief.'"

We hear, alſo, of his being preſent at the and examines pilots. examination of a French pilot, who had long frequented the Coaſt of Brazil.

There is alſo every reaſon for believing that Chart of the Rio de la Plata. the minute inſtructions for navigating the Rio de La Plata, given in Hakluyt, are from his pen.

The boy king had himſelf a great taſte for King Edward VI. ſtudies navigation. maritime affairs; when quite a child he knew all the harbours and ports in France and Scotland, as well as thoſe in his own dominions; how much water they had, and the way to get into them.

We have it on the teſtimony of the noble Venetian, Sanuto, that Cabot had explained Cabot explains to him the variation of the compaſs. " Geographia," Sanuto, lib. prim. fol. 2. Venice, 1588. to the king the whole ſubject of the variation of the needle, which Guido Gianeti, their mutual friend in London, informed Sanuto "That Sebaſtian Cabot was the firſt diſcoverer of this hid ſecret of nature; that he ſhowed the extent of the variation, and alſo that it was different in different places."

Life of

High eſteem in which Cabot is held

Gianeti reſided near to Cabot, and from him and others Sanuto learned that Cabot was held in the higheſt eſteem.

Sanuto's inſtrument.

Sanuto had conſtrudted at Venice an inſtrument for meaſuring the longitude; hence it became a matter of great importance to him to aſcertain a point of no variation.

Bartholomew Compagni's evidence as to Cabot's charts, &c.

This, after Gianeti had left England, he got from Cabot through another friend, who alſo tells him he ſaw "a chart of navigation, executed by hand with the greateſt care, and carefully compared with one made by Cabot himſelf, in which the poſition of this meridian was ſeen to be 110 miles weſt of Flores.

Sanuto proves the correctneſs of Cabot's deductions.

Sanuto remarks that he had proofs of the accuracy of the report thus made; he refers repeatedly to the map, which appears to have been ſent to him, and adverts to obſervations made by Cabot as to the variation of the compaſs at the Equator.

Where can all theſe maps, &c. be? For, beſides thoſe which Worthington's ſhade muſt anſwer for, we have at leaſt three copies traced —one each to Sanuto, Ortelius, and the Duke of Bedford, at Cheynies—to ſay nothing of

Three copies of Cabot's charts mentioned.

the extract cut by Clement Adams in this very year, 1549. Where are they? and echo alone anſwers—Where?

What Cabot's theory of the variation was we are left to conjecture; this we know, that his tranſatlantic voyages had led him to the ſcenes of its moſt marked, ſudden, and ſtriking aberrations.

It matters not that in our day Sir James Roſs has been able to reach the ſpot and indicate the exact ſite, for the time being, of the magnetic pole, which ſpot is to the eaſt of that mentioned by Cabot.

It is ever oſcillating, has no fixed reſting point; in the ſeventeenth century it was conſiderably to the eaſt of the meridian of Greenwich; in 1660 it was coincident with it, or due north and ſouth; in 1818 it had reached to 24° 30' weſt; and ſince then it has been ſlowly diminiſhing.

In an edition of Ptolemy's "Geographia," publiſhed at Rome in 1508, there is a reference to the Terra Nova and the Baccalaos, Cabot's names for the new lands, and which muſt have been taken from his charts; on a

Cabot's maps,

and his obſervations on the variation of the needle, loſt.

Change of poſition of magnetic pole.

Still oſcillating.

Cabot's approximation to its ſite, publiſhed in 1508.

map in this work is a fpot pointed out where it ftates " Here the fhips' compafs lofes its property."

Cabot's views practical, and the refult of clofe obferva- tion.

That Cabot's explanation to the king was more than a mere ftatement of ifolated facts we gather from this : he reprefented the vari- ation as differing in different places, as not abfolutely regulated by diftance from any par- ticular meridian ; that he could point to a fpot of no variation ; and that thofe whom he

He trains others to follow his fteps, and continue his examinations.

trained as feamen, as Chancellor and Stephen Burrough, were particularly attentive to this problem, noting it at one time, thrice within a fhort fpace; fo that, if his theory had been at variance with facts, his fucceffors would foon have found out the error and expofed it.

He conceives a new project. Eden's "De- cades," fol. 256.

But, though Cabot's fervices were thus dif- fufive and varied, his indomitable energy was yet to ftrike out a new enterprife, perhaps the greateft, at all events the moft fuccefsful, of his long and varied efforts. It had long been maturing in his mind, and now the time for action had come.

State of trade in England in 1551.

A general ftagnation of trade pervaded England, and a liftlefs defpondency brooded

over its commerce; ſo much ſo, that the
London merchants had an interview with the
Briſtol navigator, who "happened to be in
London," and "after much ſearch and conference together, it was at laſt concluded that
three ſhips ſhould be prepared and furniſhed
out for the ſearch and diſcovery of the northern
part of the world, to open a way and paſſage
to our men for travel to new and unknown
regions."

(1550.) Letters of incorporation were, on
the 14th of December, 1551, procured,
wherein it is declared "that, in conſideration
of his being the chiefeſt ſetter forth of this
journey, or voyage, therefore we make, ordain,
and conſtitute him, the ſaid Sebaſtian Cabot,
to be the firſt and preſent governor during his
natural life, without removal."

This was the beginning of the company of
merchant adventurers, of which our citizen
was the founder and firſt head; the Briſtol
branch was incorporated under a ſeparate charter
on December 23, 1552.

At the very outſet of the ſociety, it was to
encounter a difficulty, which would have ap-

Cabot's inter-
view with the
London
merchants.

Letters patent
of incorpora-
tion of the
merchant
adventurers'
company to
Ruſſia.
Hakluyt, vol.
i. 268.

Briſtol
charter.

palled a man of fmall mental calibre, and lèd him to give it up in defpair.

The Steelyard merchants of Germany The German cities, Antwerp and Hamburgh, held exclufive poffeffion of the trade of Northern and Central Europe. By gifts or bribes they had obtained large conceffions in the duties and cuftoms of England.

pay lefs duty on exports. They paid much lefs, for inftance, when they exported Englifh cloth, than the native manufacturer, if he chofe to export, had to pay.

They fraudulently import, In importing goods at a favoured and lower rate for themfelves, they alfo furtively introduced large quantities, as their own (for a confideration), at the low rate of duty.

Having thus fecured the command of the and monopolize the Englifh trade, crufhing the home manufacturer.
Anderfon, vol. ii. p. 90.
M'Pherfon, vol. ii. p. 109. Englifh market, as well as the monopoly of the foreign, they fet their own value on goods, and actually brought Englifh wool down to 18*d.* per ftone ; employed no Englifh fhips, and with their joint ftocks playing into each other's hands, crufhed the Englifh merchants. They were called the Stilliard (Steelyard) merchants.

Cabot's genius rofe to the occafion. He

ſaw no reaſon why, theſe impediments once removed, England ſhould not become the manufactory of the world, and her ſhips the carriers of its produce.

Cabot demurs to this;

The father of free trade, he ſet himſelf againſt this monopoly, and manfully did he battle with it.

becomes the father of free trade.

By the king's entries in his private journal we ſee the deep intereſt that Edward felt in a matter that ſo ſeriouſly concerned the welfare of his ſubjects; theſe entries are continued over five months, and are often of conſiderable length.

King Edward's deep intereſt in this matter.

At laſt, on February 23, A. D. 1551, ſucceſs crowned Cabot's perſevering efforts, and a reſult ſo auſpicious to commerce, as the breaking up of the cloſe monopoly, and ſo advantageous to the public revenue was not forgotten.

Cabot is ſucceſsful,

In March " Sebaſtian Caboto, the great ſeaman, had £200, by way of the King's Majeſty's reward."

and is rewarded by the king. Burnet's " Hiſtory Reformation," vol. ii. from the Cotton MSS.

This huge obſtacle removed, the merchant adventurers ſet to work in earneſt to open the way and paſſage to the northern ſeas.

New ſhips are ordered to be built, ſtrong

Intereſt in the new adventure.

Careful fuper-
vifion of the
new fhips.

and well-feafoned planks are felected for the purpofe, and, to guard againft the worms, "Which many times pearceth and eateth through the ftrongeft oake," it is refolved to "cover the keel of the fhippe with thinne fheets of leade."

Introduction
of the plan of
fheathing
with metal.
Hakluyt, vol.
i. p. 243.

This was the introduction of fheathing into the Britifh marine; the art had been practifed in Spain, and Cabot, if not the original inventor, muft be allowed the honour of introducing it into England.

Cabot then
living at
Briftol,

Strype tells us: "This famous expedition was fet on foot from Briftowe, where Cabot then lived."

where, pro-
bably, the
fhips were
built.

We are, therefore, juftified in fuppofing that the fhips were built on the fpot, under his perfonal fupervifion; and thus we claim for the old city the honour of being the firft place in the kingdom wherein fo ufeful an invention was practically applied.

The com-
pany on the
outlook for
information.

The adventurers were on the *qui vive* for information relating to the northern lands they wifhed to explore, wherever it could be found.

Two Tartareans employed about the king's

ſtables were brought out, and an interpreter employed to aſk them about their country, its people, manners, habits, &c. &c., but

> "Story! God blefs you, they had none to tell, firs.
>
> *   *   *   *   *   *   *   *
>
> But they'd be glad to drink their honors' health, in
> A pot of beer, if they would give them fixpence.
> For their own part, they never loved to meddle"
>
>   With fearchings.

"Being," fays the old chronicler, "more inclined to tofs pots than to learn the ſtates and difpofitions of people."

Amongſt thofe who moſt anxiouſly fought command, was Sir Hugh Willoughby, a moſt valiant and well-born gentleman, ſkilful in the fervice of war, and of a tall and commanding stature.

Eventually he was appointed to the chief command.

In command alſo of one of the ſhips, with the title of Pilot-major, was Chancellor, a perfonal friend of Cabot's, who had been brought up with Philip Sydney.

He was a ſkilful and intrepid feaman, and his remarks on the cuſtoms, religious habits,

Side notes:

Catch two Tartareans,

but get little information.

Sir Hugh Willoughby appointed to the command.

Richard Chancellor one of the captains.

Life of

manners, and laws of the countries he vifited,
prove him to have been poffeffed of great
fhrewdnefs, quick obfervation, and a highly
cultured underftanding.

His intimacy with Cabot was clofe and
reciprocal ; one incident in that great man's
hiftory, we alone know through him : viz.,
Cabot's peril in the Arctic fea through a water-
fpout.

The failing mafter in Chancellor's fhip was
Stephen Burrough, afterwards Chief Pilot of
England, and of high rank in the navy,
William Burrows, afterwards Comptroller of
the Navy, and Arthur Pet, were alfo both in
the fhip in fome fubordinate capacity.

Cabot prepared a book of inftructions, which
was ordered to be publicly read once a week
on board of each fhip. " To the intent that
every man may better remember his oath,
confcience, duty, and charge."

Thefe have been juftly regarded as model
inftructions, and reflect the higheft luftre on
his fagacity, good fenfe, and comprehenfive
knowledge.

Whilft we can only find room for a few

Margin notes:

A keen, clever man,

and perfonal friend of Cabot's. " Decades," fol. 357.

Hakluyt, vol. i. p. 233.

Cabot's excellent inftructions for the guidance and government of the expedition. Hakluyt, vol. i. p. 226.

extracts, these bits of a great man's mind will fill the reader with regret that all the records of his own Herculean labours have been loft to the world.

They are called " Ordinances, inftructions, and advertifements of and for the direction of the intended voyage to Cathay, compiled, made, and delivered by the right worfhipful M. Sebaftian Cabota, Efqr., Governour of the Myfterie and Companie of the Merchants Adventurers, for the difcoverie of regions, dominions, iflands, and places unknowen, the 9th day of May, in the yere of our Lord God 1553, and in the 7 yere of the reigne of our moft dread fovereigne Lord Edward VI., by the grace of God King of England, France, and Ireland, defender of the faith, and of the Church of England and Ireland, in earth, fupreme head."

Title of the inftructions.

" 7th item. That the merchants and other fkilful perfons, in writing, fhall daily write, defcribe, and put in memorie the navigation of each day and night, with the points and obfervations of the lands, tides, elements, altitude of the funne, courfe of the moon

" 7th item," to keep daily the log, and chronicle all paffing occurrences.

and ftarres, and the fame fo noted by the
order of the mafter and pilot of every fhip to
be put in writing ; the captaine-generall, affem-
bling the mafters together once every weeke
(if winde and weather fhall ferve) to conferre
all the obfervations and notes of the faid fhips,
to the intent it may appeare, wherein the notes
do agree and wherein they diffent, and upon
good debatement, deliberation, and conclufion,
determined to put the fame into a common
leger, to remain of record for the company ;
the like order to be kept in proportioning of
the cardes, aftrolabes, and other inftruments
prepared for the voyage, at the charge of the
companie."

Captains of
the fhips to
meet, and
compare notes
once a week.

" 27 item. The names of the people of
every ifland are to be taken in writing, with
the commodities and incommodities of the
fame ; their natures, qualities, and difpofitions, the fite of the fame, and what things
they are moft defirous of, and what commodities they will moft willingly depart
with, and what metals they have in hils,
mountains, ftreams, or rivers, in or under
the earth."

Names and
characters of
the inhabit-
ants of newly
difcovered
lands. The
production of
the countries.
&c., to be
claffified, and
taken down
in writing.

Attention to moral and religious duties is ſtrictly enjoined.

" 12 item. That no blaſpheming of God, or deteſtable ſwearing, be uſed in any ſhip, nor communication of ribaldrie, filthy tales, or ungodly talke, to be ſuffered in the company of any ſhip, neither dicing, tabling, nor other diveliſh games to be frequented, whereby enſueth not onely povertie to the players, but alſo ſtrife, variance, brauling, fighting, and oftentimes murther, to the utter deſtruction of the parties, and provoking of God's moſt juſt wrath and ſworde of vengeance. Theſe and all ſuch like peſtilences and contagions of vices and ſinnes to be eſchewed, and the offenders once moniſhed, and not reforming, to be puniſhed at the diſcretion of the captaine and maſters as appertaineth."

Swearing, filthy language, gaming, brawling, and fighting prohibited, and to be puniſhed.

" 13 item. That morning and evening prayer with other common ſervices appointed by the King's Majeſtie, and lawes of this realme, to be read and ſaide in every ſhip daily by the miniſter in the admirall, and the marchant or ſome other perſon learned in other ſhips; and the Bible or paraphraſes to

Religious duties enjoined. Morning and evening prayer, and daily reading of the Scriptures to the crew.

be read devoutly and Chriftianly to God's honour and for his grace to be obtained, and had by humble and hearty prayer of the navigants accordingly."

Public and private prayer recommended.

" 23 item. Forafmuch as our people and fhippe may appear unto them ftrange and wonderous, and theirs alfo to ours, it is to be confidered how they may be ufed, learning much of their natures and difpofitions by fome one fuch perfon as you may firft either allure or take to be brought aboard your fhippes, and there to learn as you may, *without violence or force,* and no woman to be tempted or intreated to incontinence or difhoneftie."

No violence to be ufed to the natives,

" 26 item. Every nation and region to be confidered advifedly, and not to provoke them by any diftance, laughing, contempt, or fuch like; but to ufe them with prudent circumfpection, *with all gentlenefs and courtefie;* and not to tarry long in one place until you fhall have attained the moft worthy place that may be found in fuch fort, as you may returne with victuals fufficient profperoufly."

but all Chriftian courtefy and gentlenefs to be fhewn.

In the 32nd item, he refers to the difficulties experienced from timidity and incredulity ; and ſpeaks of the " obſtacles which had miniſtered matter of ſuſpicion in ſome heads that this voyage could not ſucceed, for the extremitie of the North Pole, lacke of paſſage, and ſuch like, which have cauſed wavering minds and doubtful heads, not only to withdraw themſelves from the adventures of this voyage, but alſo diſſuaded others from the ſame," &c. &c.

Cabot draws on his own paſt experi- ence for advice to them when timid fears ariſe,

" 33rd item of inſtructions. No conſpi- racies, parttakings, factions, falſe tales, untrue reports, which be the very ſeedes and fruits of contention, diſcord, and confuſion by evil tongues, to be ſuffered, but the ſame and all other ungodlineſs to be chaſtened charitably with brotherly love, and always obedience to be uſed and practiſed by all perſons in their degrees, not only for duty and conſcience ſake towards God, under whoſe merciful hand navigants above all other creatures naturally be moſt nigh and *vicine*, but alſo for prudent and worldly policy and publick weale, con- ſidering and always having preſent in your minds that you be all one moſt loyal king's ſubjects, and naturally with daily remembrance

and adviſes thorough union.

Points out to them that they are, above all men, under God's ſpecial protection.

M

Calls to their remembrance the greatnefs of the work, the honour to themfelves and reward to their families, and the completenefs of their equipment, and devoutly prays for their fuccefs.

of the great importance of the voyage the honour, glory, praife, and benefit that depend of and upon the fame toward the common wealth of this noble realme, the advancement of you the travelers therein, your wives and children, and fo to endeavour yourfelves as that you may fatisfy the expectation of them who, at their great coftes, charges, and expenfes, have fo furnifhed you in good fort and plenty of all neceffaries as the like was never in any realme feen, ufed or known, requifite and needful for fuch an exploit, which is moft likely to be achieved and brought to good effect, if every perfon in his vocation fhall endeavour himfelf according to his charge and moft bounden duty, praying the living God to give you his grace to accomplifh your charge to his glory, whofe merciful hand fhall profper your voyage and preferve you from all dangers. In wit-

Hakluyt, vol. i, p. 227.

nefs whereof I, Sebaftian Gabota, Governor aforefaid, to thefe prefent ordinances have fubfcribed my name and put my feal the day and year above written."

Thefe inftructions do honour to the man who framed them, and prove him to have been a man of ſcience, of ſound practical buſineſs habits, and in the higheſt ſenſe of the word a Chriſtian gentleman.

CHAPTER X.

*The Expedition fails for the north-east; Chancellor's suc-
cess; Willoughby's disastrous fate; other expeditions
planned; high personages under Cabot in the company;
Chancellor's wreck and death; Muscovite Ambassador
saved; his entry into London; Cabot's opinion of liars;
his business orders to the agents; successful management
of the Company; large increase of trade. Other expeditions. The old man jubilant, gives large alms to the
poor that they may pray for the sailors; his pious com-
mendations of them to God. Dark days under Mary;
Philip of Spain lands; Cabot loses half his Pension;
gets a questionable partner in his office; antecedents of
Worthington; Cabot's maps and charts; Hakluyt not
able to get a sight of them; missing ever since; are they
in Spain now? Death-bed; says he has infallible
method of discovering the longitude. Is it the Celestial?
Summary of his life and character.*

HE fquadron was ready on the
20th of May. "The greater
fhippes are towed down with
boats and oars, and the mariners,
being all apparelled in watchett, or fkie-color'd

cloth, rowed amaine, and made way with diligence."

" And being come neare to Greenwich, where the Court then lay, prefently, upon the newes thereof, the courtiers came running out, and the common people flocked together, ſtanding very thicke upon the ſhoare ; the privie counſel, they lookt out at the windowes of the Court, and the reſt ranne up to the toppes of the towers ; the ſhippes hereupon diſcharge their ordinance and ſhoot off their peaces, after the manner of warre and of the ſea ; infomuch that the tops of the hilles founded therewith, the valleys and the waters gave an echo, and the mariners, they ſhouted in ſuch ſort that the ſkie rang againe with the noyſe thereof. One ſtood in the poope of the ſhippe, and by his geſture bids farewell to his friendes in the beſt maner hee coulde. Another walkes upon the hatches, another climbes the ſhroudes, another ſtands upon the maine yard, and another in the toppe of the ſhippe. To be ſhorte, it was a very triumph (after a ſort) in all reſpeċts to the beholders. But, alas, the good King Edward (in reſpeċt

Hakluyt, vol. i. p. 245.

Arrives at Greenwich.

Great rejoicings on ſhore, and on board the ſhips.

of whom principally all this was prepared),
hee only by reafon of ficknefs was abfent from
this fhowe, and not long after the departure
of thefe fhippes the lamentable and moft for-
rowful accident of his death followed."

King Edward,
fick and dying,
takes no part.

They put in at Harwich for final orders,
and were delayed a while ; " yet, at the lafte,
with a good winde, they hoyfted up fayle
and committed themfelves to the fea, giving
their laft adieu to their native country, which
they knew not whether they fhould ever returne
agayne to fee or not. Many of them looked
oftentimes backe and could not refraine from
teares, confidering into what hazards they
were to fall, and what uncertainties of the fea
they were to make tryall of." Chancellor
himfelf was moved. " His natural and fa-
therly affection alfo fomewhat troubled him,
for he left behinde him two little fonnes,
which were in the cafe of orphans if he fpedde
not well."

Let us follow his fortunes briefly. After
a feparation from his conforts in a great ftorm,
he reached the rendezvous in Norway, and
waited fome days in vain. Difheartening

repreſentations were made to deter him from
proceeding, but he remained "ſteadfaſt and
immutable in his reſolution to do or to die,"
and ſo he held on his courſe into the unfa-
thomable unknown.

His ſteady determina-
tion.

Rounding the North Cape, he came to "a
place where was no night at all, but a con-
tinuall light, and brightneſſe of the ſun
ſhyning clearlie upon the huge and mightie
ſea ; and havyng the benefit of this perpetual
light for certayne days, at length it pleaſed
God to bring them to a certayne bay, which
was one hundred miles or thereabouts over,
whereinto they entered ſomewhat farre and
caſt anchor."

Rounds the North Cape.

Reaches the White Sea.

Landing near Archangel, then only a caſtle,
the influence of Cabot's injunction as to gentleneſs was ſeen, and had a moſt happy reſult.

Lands on the ſpot where Archangel now ſtands.

The people at firſt, half dead with fear,
threw themſelves at Chancellor's feet ; " but
he, in a lovinge forte, did take them up from
the grounde, and this humanitie did purchaſe
to himſelf great favour through the ſpreading
abroad a report of the ſtrange people, who
were yet ſo full of ſingular gentleneſſe and

Tranquillizes the natives.

Is provifioned by them.

courtefie, whereupon the natives fupplied them
with victuals freely."

It is not the province of the writer to fol-
Journeys overland to Mofcow.
low Chancellor in his fuccefsful overland route
to Mofcow, where he had a moft cordial reception, and laid the folid foundations of a
trade which is carried on to this day.

It is with the well-won refults we have
more particularly to deal. But ere we do
this, let us for a few moments enquire as to
the fate of the gallant Willoughby.

Willoughby's expedition.
After being parted from their confort,
Chancellor, all trace of him was entirely loft;
but, though the fea fhall not give up its dead
till the Archangel's trump fhall found, the
icy kingdom does at times unlock its treafure
houfe and reveal fome dread ftory of the
paft.

His frozen-up fhips dif-covered.
Long, long afterwards the frozen-up fhips
were difcovered; of courfe, no living beings
were there; but the admiral's journal had
Some of them alive in January, 1554.
been kept, and Gabriel Willoughby's will was
attefted by brave Sir Hugh, as late as January
1554.

Hakluyt, vol. i. p. 245.
The laft entry defcribed the " Unknowen

and moſt wonderful wild beaſts aſſembling in
fearful numbers about the ſhips."

And then Oblivion in mercy draws a pall
over the ſcene; but, as one by one falls into
the arms of death, we ſeem to ſee the King of
the eternal ſnows, the Lord of the vaſt unknown, as the laſt hardy ſurvivor drops life-
leſs by the ſide of his unburied comrades,
barring afreſh the gate of his terrible domain,
whiſtling a tempeſt dirge amidſt the cryſtal
peaks of his icy mountains, and then burying
all record of the bold intruders under a mantle
of fleecy ſnow.

Their tragic fate.

What was the immediate cauſe of ſo diſmal
a cataſtrophe can now be only matter of conjecture; it could ſcarcely have been diſeaſe or
famine,—ſome note would in either caſe have
been moſt probably made in the journal; the
greater probability is, that they ſuccumbed to
the intenſe cold. Thomſon pathetically laments
their fate in the following lines :—

Probable cauſe of their death.

"Miſerable they
Who here, entangled in the gathering ice,
Take their laſt look of the deſcending ſun ;
While, full of death, and fierce with tenfold froſt,
The long, long night incumbent o'er their heads,

Falls horrible. Such was the Briton's fate,
As with firſt prow (what have not Britons dared ?)
He for the paſſage fought, attempted ſince,
So much in vain."

Cabot at
work whilſt
the expedi-
tion of
Willoughby
is away.

Cabot, whilſt the expedition was making its way towards the north, was not idle. In conjunction with Sir George Barnes, the Lord Mayor, Sheriff Garrett, who became Lord Mayor in 1555, York, Wyndham, and other adventurers, he overſees, and, on the 12th of

Organizes a
new adven-
ture to
Guinea.

Auguſt, 1553, deſpatches another expedition to Guinea, which we are told failed through the miſconduct of Captain Wyndham.

This voyage, for which the King lent two

Names of the
ſhips
employed.

ſhips, the " Primroſe," and the " Lion," pinnace, has been by Strype confounded and mixed up with the previouſly deſcribed expedition, in which we have ſeen that two of the ſhips were totally loſt, and the third we ſhall find was ſo afterwards; whereas this ſhip, the " Primroſe," was in exiſtence, and was the admiral's ſhip in 1557, in which year ſhe was choſen to carry home to Ruſſia the ambaſſador from that country, ſo that ſhe could not have formed one of this firſt expedition. Named

in the charter, and numbered amongſt the
adventurers, we have the following liſt of
high officials, compriſing the beſt blood and
higheſt rank in the kingdom. "Our right
truſty and well beloved counſellor, William,
Marquis of Wincheſter, Lord High Treaſurer"
(a Paulet, who lived to ſee 103 deſcendants
of his own body) ; "Henry, Earl of Arundel,
Lord Steward of the Houſehold ; John, Earl
of Bedford, Lord Keeper of the Privy Seal ;
William, Earl of Pembroke" (who this year
rode into London to his manſion, Baynard
Caſtle, with 300 horſe in his retinue, of which
100 of them were gentlemen in plain blue
cloth, with chains of gold and badges of a
dragon on their ſleeves) ; "William Lord
Howard, of Effingham, the Lord High Admiral of England, &c. &c. &c., all of whom
are incorporated under one Governor" (Sebaſtian Cabot, as the chiefeſt ſetter forth of
the enterpriſe) "of the ſaid fellowſhip and
community of merchants adventurers, for the
diſcovery of lands, territories, iſles, dominions,
and ſeigniories, unknowen, and not before
that late adventure by ſea commonly fre-

Hakluyt, vol.
i. p. 267.

Noble mem-
bers of the
company who
ſerved with
and under
Governor
Cabot.

quented; which, by the fufferance and grace
of Almighty God, it fhall chaunce them failing
northwards, north eaftwards, or north-weft-
wards, to finde and attain, by their faid adventure," &c. &c. &c.

Thefe extenfive fchemes of commerce and
difcovery were overfhadowed by the domeftic
broils which foon followed, feparating the noble
adventurers into virulent oppofing factions.

Mary's hufband, Philip of Spain, to ferve
his own purpofes, managed to embroil this
country in a war with France, which ftill further deranged the ambitious views of the
company, fo that their own attempts were re-
ftricted to their firft, or Ruffian fpeculation, to
which we now return very briefly.

Chancellor obtained from the Emperor of
Ruffia a charter to Sebaftian Cabota, Governor,
Sir George Barnes, Knight, &c., Confuls, Sir
John Grefham, and others, affiftants, and to
the " commonaltie of the aforenamed fellow-
fhip " and to their fucceffors for ever, &c. &c.,
containing certain privileges which placed
their future commercial intercourfe upon the
moft liberal and fecure footing.

Inteftine broils break up the adventurers to a large extent.

Philip of Spain, by his policy, hinders an extenfion of their plans.

Chancellor gets a charter for Governor Cabot to trade with Ruffia.

On a ſubſequent voyage of Chancellor's the Emperor ſent back with him Oſep Nepea Gregorowitch, as his orator or ambaſſador, together with four ſhips heavily laden with furs, wax, train-oil, and other Ruſſian commodities, to the value of upwards of £20,000, which belonged partly to the merchants and partly to the orator; two of theſe ſhips were wrecked on the coaſt of Norway—one reached the Thames in ſafety; but the "Edward Bonaventure," Chancellor's own ſhip, was driven on the rocks at Pitſligo, in Scotland, and the intrepid Grand Pilot (which Chancellor now by appointment had become), whilſt trying to ſave the ambaſſador and ſeven of his attendants in his own boat, periſhed cloſe to the land.

"The noble ambaſſador being, by God's preſervation and of ſpecial favour, with a fewe others, only withe much difficultie, ſaved."

As ſoon as the ſad tidings reached London, proviſion was made for the wants of the ſhipwrecked Muſcovite; and on his approach to London, on the 27th of February, 1557, he was met, twelve miles out of the city, by

The Emperor of Ruſſia ſends, by Chancellor, an ambaſſador to England in 1556, when Chancellor is wrecked, but ſaves the ambaſſador's life at the coſt of his own.

The ambaſſador draws near London, fourſcore merchants, with chains of gold and goodly apparel, with an array of menſervants in one uniform livery, upon good horſes and geldings, who conducted him to a merchant's houſe four miles from London, and ſupplying him with gold, velvet, ſilk, and all furniture requiſite; he had a riding garment made for him by the next day.

and is met by a royal cavalcade, and one hundred and forty merchant adventurers on horſeback with Governor Cabot. Then the merchants adventuring for Ruſſia, to the number of *one hundred and forty perſons*, and ſo many or more ſervants in one livery, conducted him towards the City of London, ſhowing him by the way the hunting of the fox, and many other ſuch like ſports. The Right Honourable Viſcount Montague, a ſpecial meſſenger from the Queen, here met and embraced him by commandment, and, with three hundred knights and gentlemen, accompanied him to London; at the north part of which, four notable merchants preſented to him a right fair and large gelding, richly trapped, together with a foot-cloth of orient crimſon velvet, enriched with gold lace, all furniſhed in the moſt glorious faſhion, the preſent gift of the ſaid merchants.

At Smithfield Bars the Lord Mayor and Aldermen in ſcarlet received him, and ſo preceded by the merchants and notable perſonages, and riding between the Lord Mayor and Lord Montague, with a large troop of ſervants and apprentices following, he was conducted to his lodgings in "Fantchurchſtreet, with greate admiration and plauſibilitie of the people, running plentifullie on all ſides, and replenyſhinge all ſtreetes in ſuch ſort as no man without difficultie might paſſe." Here, in "two chambers richly hanged and decked, with an ample rich cupboard of plate," he abode until the 3rd of May, receiving many aldermen and the graveſt perſonages of the ſaid company, who provided for his table as appertayned to an ambaſſador of ſuch honour."

But the wary old Governor had ſeen foreigners before, and in their own homes, and he ſeems very ſoon to have "Scratched the ſkin and diſcovered the Tartar;" for, writing to their agents in Ruſſia ſoon after Oſep's arrival, he ſays :—

" Wee doe not finde the ambaſſadour nowe

Marginal notes:

At the City bounds the Lord Mayor and Corporation meet, and give him welcome.

His lodging.

Cabot looks beneath the ſurface,

and records
his opinion
of the
ambaſſador.

at the laſt ſo conformable to reaſon as wee
had thought wee ſhoulde. Hee is very miſ-
truſtfull and thinketh every man will beguile
him. Therefore you had neede to take heede
howe you have to doe with him, or with any
ſuch, and to make your bargains plaine, and
to ſet them downe in writing. For they be
ſubtill people, and doe not alwaies ſpeake the
truth, and thinke other men toe be like themſelves; therefore we would have none of them
to ſend any goods in our ſhips at any time,
nor none to come for paſſengers."

Cabot a lover
of truth.

Riches, honours, and high poſitions, had
not ſpoiled the old Briſtol mariner; truth
and he had ſhaken hands, and were boſom
friends now; he doeſn't like a liar, even
though he repreſent an emperor; "ſo pray
don't let any more of that ſort come into
England—the ſample is enough—keep out
the bulk."

The trade
with Ruſſia
on the
increaſe.

Meanwhile the trade increaſes; in 1557
four ſhips ſail for Ruſſia—one of them the
"Primroſe," carrying the ambaſſador, the
maſter of which ſhip, "under God, was John
Buckland," theſe were all laden with cloths,

cottons, and pewter. Seven rope-makers were
ſent out to work up the raw flax and hemp,
and to teach the trade to the natives, ſo that
when theſe return, " we may not be deſtitute
of good workmen, for we eſteem this a principal commoditie, and that *the counſel of England doth well allowe.*"

Ten young men, as apprentices, went out
alſo in the fleet, who were to be appointed to
various offices and places, to keep accounts,
to buy and ſell, or to go as agents to notable
cities of the country, for obſervation, underſtanding, and knowledge.

They alſo ſent a ſkinner " to view and ſee
ſuch furs as you ſhall cheape or buy," but
they inſtruct them " that ſables, and ſuch rich
furs as they, bee not every man's money, and
ſo ſend but few."

Underſtanding alſo " that. in Permia and
Ugory there is great quantity of yewe, which
is a ſpecial commoditie for our realme," they
ſend out Leonard Brian " to 'ſhewe how it
ſhould be cut down and cloven."

The chief return in lading was to be of
" wexe, flaxe, tallow, and trayne oil, and in

Hakluyt, vol.
i. p. 297.

Teaches the
natives rope-
making, by
advice of the
Privy Counci::

Apprentices
taken to learn
the duties of
agents.

Skinner ſen:
to choſe the
right ſort of
furs,

and a bowyer
to ſeleɛt yew
for bows.

future voyages they were to add cables, ropes, and linen yarn."

Tartar fteel the beft.

They are alfo to look out for the fteel of the Tartars, which is faid to be better than the Ruffian, and both of them very plentiful.

Copper plentiful.

To keep their eye alfo on the copper of the country, " either in plates or round cakes, for of that alfo there is faid to be great plenty ;" and to fend fpecimens of every commodity in the country, as famples.

Ruffia leather, and the dyes ufed in its manufacture.

Efpecially were they to be mindful of this in the matter of leather; " alfo of the herbs, earth, or whatfoever the Ruffians dye with, and to be fure and fend famples of what they get for that purpofe from the Turks and the Tartars."

They were alfo to note well what Englifh goods beft fuited the different parts of the vaft

To note the weights and meafures; alfo the goods that fuit, and the value of the money.

country, and to " certify how their weights and meafures do anfwer to ours ; alfo to fend over three roubles in money, that we may try the juft value of them." (This inveftment will certainly not break the company.)

Another letter advifes the buying up of the wax by the company, as it is plentiful and cheap. "A good and ſafe article for the realme, ſo that, having it wholly in our hands, we may ſerve our own country and others, and ſo to pay for it, that it may not be on their hands who have it to ſell."

Adviſes the buying up of all the wax.

The wax chandlery in thoſe days was one of the wealthieſt trades in the kingdom.

One hundred and forty tuns of caſks in ſtaves were now ſent for the oil, and all the agents were directed to correſpond regularly with head-quarters at Moſcow, and to keep the merchant there well poſted up in all matters relating to the country, its wants, and the trade of their ſeveral ſtations, "that he may give us large inſtructions, as well what is ſolde and boughte, as alſo what lading we ſhall take ; alſo what kind of goods we ſhall ſend.

Caſks in ſtaves ſent for oil.

" For we muſt procure to utter good quantity of wares, eſpecially thoſe of our own realm, although we afford *a good pennyworth*, to the intent to make other that have traded thitherto weary, and ſo to bring ourſelves and our goods into eſtimation, and likewiſe to procure and have the chief commodities of

Adviſes the under-ſelling all other nations.

that country in our hands—as waxe, and fuch others, that other nations may be ferved by us and at our hands."

They are alfo inftructed to write in cypher all letters which they fend overland ; but with the fhips they are to fend home one of their moft intelligent young men (Arthur Edwards is named), "to certify us in any doubts, whom we will remit to you again in the next fhip."

Nor is the energy and bufinefs tact, here difplayed by the worfhipful and worthy old governor, confined to him or to his company.

The whaling trade to Spitzbergen owes its origin to their difcovery, and was foon carried on with good refults.

An impulfe had been given to England which quickened its commerce, and refulted

in expeditions, which were fent in different directions in this and the following reign.

And all this change is due, "under God," as they ever pioufly fay, to the found advice which, in their hour of deepeft depreflion of trade, was given to them by the great Briftol feaman, and to the wifdom with which he governed the company, as feen in his feveral rules and orders.

His genius, indeed, not only quickened its commerce to life, but his paternal care nouriſhed it to its manhood.

Soon there grew up an extenfive eftabliſhment in Mofcow, for, in 1571, when the Tartars forced the city and gave all to the flames (fave the kremlin into which the Czar had retired), many Engliſhmen in the fervice of the company periſhed. *Mofcow burnt.*

In one houfe, it is faid, "twenty-five Engliſhmen periſhed in one beer-cellar, and yet in that fame cellar Rafe, his wife, John Brown, and John Clarke were preferved, which was wonderful." *Twenty-five Engliſhmen periſh in one cellar.*

It had happened that on Chancellor's firft vifit to Mofcow he met with an unexpected friend in the "Ambaſſador from the Kinge of Perfia, called the great Sophie," who was all clothed in rich fcarlet, and who fpoke to the Emperor of our men, of whofe kingdom and trade he was not ignorant. *Chancellor's friend from Perfia at Mofcow.*

This interview led to the miſſion to Perfia of Antony Jenkinfon, and the opening up of *Miſſion to Perfia.*

a trade with that kingdom, where we are informed, fays Cabot's correfpondent, " that raw
filke is as plentiful as flax in Ruffia."

Laft fketch
of Cabot.

We get one more, and that a life-like
fketch, almoft a photograph, of the old man
jubilant, ere the curtain falls, and fhuts him
into the *Forever*.

The " Sea-
thrift," Capt.
Stephen
Burroughs,
fitted out
for the north.

Stephen Burroughs, who had been with
Chancellor, was again defpatched to the north,
in 1556, in a pinnace called the " Seathrift,"
and in his journal he gives us a glimpfe of
the anxious fupervifion of Cabot, and of his
unwillingnefs to quit them until the very laft
moment of their failing.

We catch the genial fmile, marvel at the
wonderful unbroken fpirit, and note how the

Cabot's judg-
ment of
character.

wife old man gauged and underftood the character of thofe who furrounded him, and knew
how to leave a lafting impreffion on their
minds that there would ever be a feeling of
warm and loving fympathy cherifhed for them,
though far, far away, by thofe who were compelled to ftay at home.

" On the 27th of April, being Monday,
the Right Worfhipful Sebaftian Caboto came

aboord our pinneſſe at Gravefend, accompanied with divers gentlemen and gentlewomen, who, after that they had viewed our pinneſſe, and taſted of ſuch cheere as wee could make them aboarde, they went on ſhore, giveing to our marriners right liberal rewardes. And the goode olde gentleman, Maſter Cabota, gave to the poore moſt liberall almes, wiſhing them to praye for the good fortune and proſperous ſucceſſe of the ' Serchthrift,' our pinneſſe.

He, with divers others, gives the mariners a feaſt at Gravefend.

" And then, at the ſign of the Chriſtopher, he and his friends banketted, and made me and them that were in the companie great cheere ; and, for very joy that he had to ſee the towardneſſe of our intended diſcovery, he enter'd into the dance himſelf, amongſt the reſt of the younge and luſty company ; which being ended, hee and his friends departed, moſt gently commending us to the govern-ance of Almighty God."

Enters joy-fully into their fports, and, com-mending them to God, bids them farewell.

Sixty and one years have rolled away ſince the date of the firſt patent, under which Cabot failed and found a new world ; and green, vigorous, and cheerful is the ripe old age to which he has attained.

Sixty-one years ſince the firſt patent in fearch of the new lan.l.

But, alas! Queen Mary did not love thofe who had been the friends of her brother.

Her hufband, Philip of Spain, who threatened and dunned her into a war with France, who withheld the meagre penfion from a father who had given to him an empire, came to England May 20th, 1557.

Sebaftian Cabot had, as we have feen, left the fervice of Philip's father, and refufed to return. He was now imparting to others the benefit of his fkill and experience, and making England the fuccefsful rival of Spain upon the ocean.

Thofe who have ftudied the character of that monarch will not think it a ftrange coincidence that, on the 27th, or juft one week after the King's landing on Englifh fhores, the great feaman, who had fet his father at

nought, had, under preffure, to refign his office and penfion, granted to him for life by King Edward VI.

Two days afterwards William Worthington was affociated with him in the office, to which he was reinftated, and he alfo took half the old man's penfion.

All that we know previouſly of this Wor- His previous charaĉter.
thington is, that he was a defaulter in the days
of King Edward, who forgave him a conſiderable amount, of which he ſaid he had been
robbed by a runaway ſervant.

This man had now the cuſtody of Cabot's He has charge of Cabot's maps, &c.
" maps, charts, and diſcourſes, written with
his own hand," by virtue of the office into
which he had been foiſted.

Such documents would be ſecured by Philip
at any price. He had put Worthington into
the office, and ——. Well, the reader may
draw his own concluſion.

We ſhould be glad if Spain, rejoicing in Are they in Spain ?
her newly-found liberty, would let us look at
them if ſhe can. We accuſe no one, but we
have a deep ſuſpicion that they may yet be
found amongſt her archives.

Hakluyt, to whoſe taſte and reſearch our
naval hiſtory owes ſo much, though now and
then, as in Cabot's caſe, he took liberties
with the text, and, as he thought, correĉted
paſſages where he deemed the original, from
which he tranſlated, was wrong, erring only
in his judgment. Hakluyt, twenty years after

Cabot's death, ere he himfelf was made a prebendary of Briftol, tried often, he tells us,
to get a fight of this precious collection of
Cabot's, and met with repeated and peremptory refufals from Worthington, for which
there appears to have been no adequate mo-
tive. And hence, in the preface to his great
and valuable work, Hakluyt fays that "the
office of pilot-major was, not long after
Cabot's death, to the great hindrance of the
commonwealth, miferably turned to other private ufes."

Henceforth we lofe fight of the good old
man. " Ingratitude, more ftrong than traitor's
arms, quite vanquifhed him ; then burft his
mighty heart."

His faithful and attached friend, Richard
Eden, juft beckons us to fee him die.
It is with fomething like awe we gather
round the bed and find " the ruling paflion
ftrong in death." " As the fpirit ftruggles
with the clay," " he fpeaks flightily about a
Divine revelation to him of a new and infallible method of finding the longitude, which
he could not difclofe to any mortal."

Perchance Eden underſtood him not, and the dying man was thinking of Him "who, as far as the eaſt is from the weſt, hath ſo far removed our tranſgreſſions from us." In the infinite ocean of the love of his Saviour he found no variation, but a ſolid data, from which neither length, or breadth, or depth, or height could ſeparate him; which, paſſing all human underſtanding, was partially revealed in the glimpſe which his dying eye caught of the Spirit World, beyond the river, and ſo, joyouſly and truſtfully, like a child in his old age, he ſank to his reſt.

Cabot finds the Celeſtial longitude.

At even-tide it was light.

The date of his death, like that of his birth, is unknown, and we can only infer that it was in or near London, from the faﬅ that Eden, who lived there, was preſent.

Date of his death un-known,

Even where his aſhes lie is a myſtery; and he who gave to England a continent, and to Spain an empire, lies in ſome unknown tomb.

or the place of his burial.

He created our navy and made it into a profeſſion, in which, at firſt, landſmen and commanders of eminence on ſhore—like Sir Hugh Willoughby—were promoted to high

Summary of his labours for the Britiſh navy.

ſtation. But it was ſoon ſeen to be, not only highly deſirable, but abſolutely neceſſary that ſeamen ſhould, from boyhood, be trained for future command on the deep, and that every commander of a ſhip ſhould be a thorough ſailor.

Campbell's opinion of Cabot.

Campbell terms him the author of our maritime ſtrength; and it is impoſſible for even the moſt curſory reader of theſe pages to be blind to the immenſe ſervices which he rendered to this nation, whoſe power and poſition in the world have been won by her commerce and her ſhips.

His diſcoveries,

This man, who ſurveyed and depicted three thouſand miles of a coaſt which he had diſcovered; who gave to Britain, not only the

labours,

continent, but the untold riches of the deep, in the fiſheries of Newfoundland, and the whale fiſhery of the Arctic Sea; who broke

wiſdom,

up a monopoly that, vampire-like, was ſucking out England's infant ſtrength, and unlocked for her the treaſures of the world, ſaying, " Go, win and then wear them ;" who is never re-

gentleneſs,

ported to have ſtruck an aggreſſive blow; who made enemies into friends, and whoſe friends were ever warmly attached to him; who, by his uprightneſs and fair dealing, raiſed England's name high among the nations, placed her credit on a ſolid foundation, and made her citizens reſpected; who was the father of free trade, and gave us the carrying trade of the world: this man has not a ſtatue in the city that gave him birth, or in the metropolis of the country he ſo greatly enriched, or a name on the land he diſcovered. Emphatically, the moſt ſcientific ſeaman of his own or, perhaps, many ſubſequent ages—one of the gentleſt, braveſt, beſt of men—his actions have been miſrepreſented, his diſcoveries denied, his deeds aſcribed to others, and calumny has flung its filth on his memory.

We have ſtriven to clear away the miſrepreſentations with which ignorance, prejudice, and malignity have overlaid his life and actions, and to bring out the man from the ſhroud in which oblivion had partially enwrapped him.

To us it has been indeed a labour of love; for, like ſome glorious antique in an acropolis of weeds, he grew in beauty as we lifted off,

and high and honourable character, a public gain to England, and the ſeed whence ſprang our commercial greatneſs.

This a labour of love,

one after another, the aſperſions which had been caſt upon him, until, as the laſt ſtain was removed, and our loving work was done, as he ſtood before us in the majeſty of his true manhood, we were amazed that ſuch a man ſhould have remained ſo little known, and our only ſorrow in connection with our work was this—that the taſk of exhuming his reputation had not fallen into abler and more efficient hands.

VALE.

PRINTED BY WHITTINGHAM AND WILKINS,
TOOKS COURT, CHANCERY LANE.

A List of Books

!PUBLISHING BY

SAMPSON LOW, SON, AND MARSTON,

Crown Buildings, 188, Fleet Street.

[*March*, 1869.

NEW ILLUSTRATED WORKS.

N ELEGY IN A COUNTRY CHURCHYARD. By
Thomas Gray. With Sixteen Water-Colour Drawings, by
Eminent Artists, printed in Colours in facsimile of the Ori-
ginals. Uniform with the Illustrated " Story Without an End."
Royal 8vo. cloth, 12s. 6d.; or in morocco. 25s.

" *Another edition of the immortal ' Elegy,' charmingly printed and
gracefully bound, but with a new feature. The illustrations are woodcuts
in colours, and they are admirable specimens of the art.*"—Art Journal.
" *Remarkable for thoughtful conception and all that artistic finish of which
this newly-born art is capable.*"—Morning Post. "*Beauty and care visible
throughout.*"—Standard.

THE STORY WITHOUT AN END. From the German of
Carové. By Sarah Austin. Illustrated with Sixteen Original Water-
Colour Drawings by E. V. B., printed in Fac-simile and numerous Illus-
trations on wood. Small 4to. cloth extra, 12s.; or in morocco, 21s.

* ** Also a Large Paper Edition, with the Plates mounted (only 250
copies printed), morocco, ivory inlaid, 31s. 6d.

" *Nowhere will he find the Book of Nature more freshly and beautifully
opened for him than in ' The Story without an End,' of its kind one of the
best that was ever written.*"—Quarterly Review.

Also, illustrated by the same Artist.

Child's Play. Printed in fac-simile from Water-Colour Drawings, 7s. 6d.
Tennyson's May Queen. Illustrated on Wood. Large Paper Edit. 7s. 6d.

PEAKS AND VALLEYS OF THE ALPS. From Water-
colour Drawings by Elijah Walton. Chromo-Lithographed by J. H.
Lowes, with Descriptive Text by the Rev. T. G. Bonney, M. A., F.G.S.
Folio, half morocco, with 21 large Plates. Original subscription 8
guineas. A very limited edition only now issued at 4l. 14s. 6d.

The Seven Churches of Asia. The result of Two Years' Exploration of their Locality'and Remains. By Mr. A. Svoboda. With 20 full-
page Photographs taken on the spot. Edited with a preface by the Rev.
H. B. Tristram, F.L.S. 4to. cloth extra, price 2 guineas.

"*Some time since we reviewed the photographs taken by Mr. Svoboda
on the sites of the famous Christian cities of Asia Minor, and found in
them much that was interesting to the Biblical student and historian. We
have in the well-printed volume before us twenty of these interesting illustrations, which fairly display the present state of the ruins so deeply connected
with the early history of Christianity. Of these Smyrna supplies four,
Ephesus five, Laodicea two, Hieropolis one, Sardis two, Philadelphia one,
Magnesia Sypilusone, Thyatira one, and Pergamos three. To these the
author has attached a carefully-written and very interesting series of
accounts of the ruins and their history, taken from a popular and Scrip-
tural point of view. Mr. Tristram has done his share of the work well,
and edited a capital manual which is suited not only to general readers,
but as a book of reference on a subject about which little is known, and
that little not available without researches which would rival those of our
author.*"—Athenæum.

Christian Lyrics. Chiefly selected from Modern Authors. 138
Poems, illustrated with upwards of 150 Engravings, under the superintendence of J. D. Cooper. Small 4to. cloth extra, 10s. 6d.; morocco, 21s.

Illustrations of the Natural Order of Plants; with Groups and
Descriptions. By Elizabeth Twining. Splendidly illustrated in colours
from nature. Reduced from the folio edition. 2 vols. Royal 8vo. cloth
extra, price 5 guineas.

Choice Editions of Choice Books. New Editions. Illustrated by
C. W. Cope, R.A., T. Creswick, R.A., Edward Duncan, Birket Foster,
J. C. Horsley, A. R. A., George Hicks, R. Redgrave, R.A., C. Stonehouse,
F. Tayler, George Thomas, H. J. Townshend, E. H. Wehnert, Har-
rison Weir, &c. Crown 8vo. cloth, 5s. each; mor. 10s. 6d.

Bloomfield's Farmer's Boy.	Keat's Eve of St. Agnes.
Campbell's Pleasures of Hope.	Milton's l'Allegro.
Cundall's Elizabethan Poetry.	Rogers' Pleasures of Memory.
Coleridge's Ancient Mariner.	Shakespeare's Songs and Sonnets.
Goldsmith's Deserted Village.	Tennyson's May Queen.
Goldsmith's Vicar of Wakefield.	Weir's Poetry of Nature.
Gray's Elegy in a Churchyard.	Wordsworth's Pastoral Poems.

Bishop Heber's Hymns. An Illustrated Edition, with upwards
of one hundred Designs. Engraved, in the first style of Art under the
superintendence of J. D. Cooper. Small 4to. handsomely bound, price
Half a Guinea; morocco, 21s.

The Divine and Moral Songs of Dr. Watts: a New and very
choice Edition. Illustrated with One Hundred Woodcuts in the first
style of the Art, from Original Designs by Eminent Artists; engraved
by J. D. Cooper. Small 4to. cloth extra, price 7s. 6d.; morocco, 15s.

Light after Darkness: Religious Poems by Harriet Beecher
Stowe. With Illustrations. Small post 8vo. cloth, 3s. 6d.

Artists and Arabs; or Sketching in Sunshine. By Henry
Blackburn, author of "The Pyrenees," &c. Numerous Illustrations.
Demy 8vo. cloth. 10s. 6d.

The Pyrenees; 100 Illustrations by Gustave Doré, and a Description of Summer Life at French Watering Places By Henry Blackburn. Royal 8vo. cloth, 18s. ; morocco, 25s.

Also by the same Author.

TRAVELLING IN SPAIN, illustrated, 16s. or Cheaper Edition, 6s.

Milton's Paradise Lost. With the original Steel Engravings of
John Martin. Printed on large paper, royal 4to. handsomely bound,
3l. 13s. 6d. ; morocco extra, 5l. 15s. 6d.

Favourite English Poems. *Complete Edition.* Comprising a
Collection of the most celebrated Poems in the English Language, with
but one or two exceptions unabridged, from Chaucer to Tennyson. With
300 Illustrations by the first Artists. Two vols. royal 8vo. half bound,
top gilt, Roxburgh style, 1l. 18s. ; antique calf, 3l. 3s.

Schiller's Lay of the Bell. Sir E. Bulwer Lytton's translation ;
beautifully illustrated by forty-two wood Engravings, drawn by Thomas
Scott, and engraved by J. D. Cooper, after the Etchings by Retszch.
Oblong 4to. cloth extra, 14s. ; morocco, 25s.

Edgar A. Poe's Poems. Illustrated by Eminent Artists. Small
4to. cloth extra, price 10s. 6d.

A New and Revised Edition of Mrs. Palliser's Book of Lace,
comprising a History of the Fabric from the Earliest Period, with upwards of 100 Illustrations and Coloured Designs, including some Interesting Examples from the Leeds Exhibition. By Mrs. Bury Palliser.
1 vol. 8vo. cloth extra. [*Nearly ready.*

The Royal Cookery Book. By Jules Gouffé, Chef de Cuisine of
the Paris Jockey Club. Translated and Adapted for English use. By
Alphonse Gouffé, Head Pastrycook to Her Majesty the Queen. Illustrated with large Plates beautifully printed in Colours, and One Hundred and Sixty-One Woodcuts. Super-royal 8vo. cloth extra, 2l. 2s.

. *Notice—Household Cheaper Edition.*—The unanimous welcome ac-
corded to " The Royal Cookery Book " by all the leading reviews within
the short time that has elapsed since its appearance, and the conviction
that it is *the cookery book for the age,* induce the Publishers to issue
for contemporaneous sale with this sumptuous presentation volume a
Household Edition in one handsome large type book for domestic use.
Price 10s. 6d., strongly half-bound.

The Bayard Series.

CHOICE COMPANIONABLE PLEASURE BOOKS OF LITERATURE
FOR CIRCULATION AT HOME AND ABROAD,
COMPRISING
HISTORY, BIOGRAPHY, TRAVEL, ESSAYS, NOVELETTES, ETC.

Which, under careful editing, will be very choicely printed, with Vignette Title-page, Notes, and Index ; the aim being to insure permanent value, as well as present attractiveness, and to render each volume an acquisition to the libraries of a new generation of readers. 16mo. bound flexible in cloth extra, gilt edges, with silk head bands and registers.

Each Volume, complete in itself, price Half-a-crown.

THE STORY OF THE CHEVALIER BAYARD. From the French of the Loyal Servant, M. de Berville, and others. By E. Walford. With Introduction and Notes by the Editor.

> " Praise of him must walk the earth
> For ever, and to noble deeds give birth.
> This is the happy warrior ; this is he
> That every man in arms would wish to be."— *Wordsworth.*

SAINT LOUIS, KING OF FRANCE. The curious and characteristic Life of this Monarch by De Joinville. Translated by James Hutton.

> " *St. Louis and his companions, as described by Joinville, not only in their glistening armour, but in their every-day attire, are brought nearer to us, become intelligible to us, and teach us lessons of humanity which we can learn from men only, and not from saints and heroes. Here lies the real value of real history. It widens our minds and our hearts, and gives us that true knowledge of the world and of human nature in all its phases which but few can gain in the short span of their own life, and in the narrow sphere of their friends and enemies. We can hardly imagine a better book for boys to read or for men to ponder over.*"—Times.

THE ESSAYS OF ABRAHAM COWLEY. Comprising all his Prose Works ; the Celebrated Character of Cromwell, Cutter of Coleman Street, &c. &c. With Life, Notes, and Illustrations.

> " *Praised in his day as a great Poet ; the head of the school of poets called metaphysical, he is now chiefly known by those prose essays, all too short, and all too few, which, whether for thought or for expression, have rarely been excelled by any writer in any language.*"—Mary Russell Mitford's Recollections.

ABDALLAH AND THE FOUR-LEAVED SHAMROCK. By Edouard Laboullaye, of the French Academy. Translated by Mary L. Booth.

> *One of the noblest and purest French stories ever written.*

The Bayard Series,—

TABLE-TALK AND OPINIONS OF NAPOLEON THE FIRST.

A compilation from the best sources of this great man's shrewd and often prophetic thoughts, forming the best inner life of the most extraordinary man of modern times.

THE KING AND THE COMMONS : Cavalier and Puritan

Poems. Selected and Arranged by Henry Morley, Professor of Literature, London University.

** It was in working on this volume that Mr. Morley discovered the New Poem attributed to Milton. A facsimile of the Poem and Signature J. or P. M., with parallel passages, and the whole of the evidence, pro and con, is given in the prefatory matter.

VATHEK. An Oriental Romance. By William Beckford.

" Beckford's ' Vathek ' is here presented as one of the beautifully got-up works included in Messrs. Low and Co.'s ' Bayard Series,' every one of which is a gem, and the ' Caliph Vathek ' is, perhaps, the gem of the collection."—Illustrated Times.

WORDS OF WELLINGTON. Maxims and Opinions, Sen-

tences and Reflections, of the Great Duke, gathered from his Despatches, Letters and Speeches. Printed at the Chiswick Press, on toned paper, cloth extra, price 2s. 6d.

" One of the best books that could be put into the hands of a youth to influence him for good."—Notes and Queries.

RASSELAS, PRINCE OF ABYSSINIA. By Dr. Johnson.

With Introduction by the Rev. William West, B.A.

" We are glad to welcome a reprint of a little book which a great master of English prose once said, ' will claim perhaps the first place in English composition for a model of grave and majestic language.' It contains so many grave maxims, so many hints as to the conduct of life, and so much vigorous and suggestive thought, and shrewd insight into the follies and frailties, the greatness and weakness of human nature, that it is just one of those books which, like ' Bacon's Essays,' we read again and again with ever-increasing profit and pleasure."—Examiner

" ' The Bayard Series ' is a perfect marvel of cheapness and of exquisite taste in the binding and getting up. We hope and believe that these delicate morsels of choice literature will be widely and gratefully welcomed."—Nonconformist   *" Every one of the works included in this series is well worth possessing, and the whole will make an admirable foundation for the library of a studious youth of polished and refined tastes."*—Illustrated Times.   *" We have here two more volumes of the series appropriately called the ' Bayard,' as they certainly are ' sans reproche.' Of convenient size, with clear typography, and tasteful binding, we know no other little volumes which make such good gift books for persons of mature age."*—Examiner.   *" If the publishers go on as they have begun, they will have furnished us with one of the most valuable and attractive series of books that have ever been issued from the press."*—Sunday Times.   *" There has, perhaps, never been produced anything more admirable, either as regards matter or manner."*—Oxford Times.

The Gentle Life Series.

Printed in Elzevir, on Toned Paper, and handsomely bound,
forming suitable Volumes for Presents.

Price 6s. each; or in calf extra, price 10s. 6d.

I.

THE GENTLE LIFE. Essays in Aid of the Formation of
Character of Gentlemen and Gentlewomen. Ninth Edition.

> "*His notion of a gentleman is of the noblest and truest order. The
> volume is a capital specimen of what may be done by honest reason,
> high feeling, and cultivated intellect. A little compendium of cheerful
> philosophy.*"—Daily News. "*Deserves to be printed in letters of gold,
> and circulated in every house.*"—Chambers's Journal. "*The writer's
> object is to teach people to be truthful, sincere, generous: to be humble-
> minded, but bold in thought and action.*"—Spectator. "*It is with the more
> satisfaction that we meet with a new essayist who delights without the
> smallest pedantry to quote the choicest wisdom of our forefathers, and
> who abides by those old-fashioned Christian ideas of duty which Steele and
> Addison, wits and men of the world, were not ashamed to set before the
> young Englishmen of 1713.*"—London Review.

II.

ABOUT IN THE WORLD. Essays by the Author of "The
Gentle Life."

> "*It is not easy to open it at any page without finding some happy idea.*"
> Morning Post. "*Another characteristic merit of these essays is, that they
> make it their business, gently but firmly, to apply the qualifications and the
> corrections, which all philanthropic theories, all general rules or maxims, or
> principles, stand in need of before you can make them work.*"—Literary
> Churchman.

III.

LIKE UNTO CHRIST. A new translation of the "De Imita-
tione Christi," usually ascribed to Thomas à Kempis. With a Vignette
from an Original Drawing by Sir Thomas Lawrence. Second Edition.

> "*Think of the little work of Thomas à Kempis, translated into a hundred
> languages, and sold by millions of copies, and which, in inmost moments
> of deep thought, men make the guide of their hearts, and the friend of
> their closets.*"—Archbishop of York, at the Literary Fund, 1865.
> "*Evinces independent scholarship, a profound feeling for the original,
> and a minute attention to delicate shades of expression, which may well
> make it acceptable even to those who can enjoy the work without a trans-
> lator's aid.*"—Nonconformist. "*Could not be presented in a more exquisite
> form, for a more sightly volume was never seen.*"—Illustrated London
> News. "*The preliminary essay is well-written, good, and interesting.*"—
> Saturday Review.

IV.

FAMILIAR WORDS. An Index Verborum, or Quotation Handbook. Affording an immediate Reference to Phrases and Sentences that have become embedded in the English language. Second and enlarged Edition.

"*Should be on every library table, by the side of ' Roget's Thesaurus.' *"—Daily News. "*Almost every familiar quotation is to be found in this work, which forms a book of reference absolutely indispensable to the literary man, and of interest and service to the public generally. Mr. Friswell has our best thanks for his painstaking, laborious, and conscientious work.*"—City Press.

V.

ESSAYS BY MONTAIGNE. Edited, Compared, Revised, and Annotated by the Author of "The Gentle Life." With Viguette Portrait. Second Edition.

"*We should be glad if any words of ours could help to bespeak a large circulation for this handsome attractive book; and who can refuse his homage to the good-humoured industry of the editor.*"—Illustrated Times. "*The reader really gets in a compact form all of the charming, chatty Montaigne that he needs to know.*"—Observer. "*This edition is pure of questionable matter, and its perusal is calculated to enrich without corrupting the mind of the reader.*"—Daily News.

VI.

THE COUNTESS OF PEMBROKE'S ARCADIA. Written by Sir Philip Sidney. Edited, with Notes, by the Author of "The Gentle Life." Dedicated, by permission, to the Earl of Derby. 7s. 6d.

"*All the best things in the Arcadia are retained intact in Mr. Friswell's edition, and even brought into greater prominence than in the original, by the curtailment of some of its inferior portions, and the omission of most of its eclogues and other metrical digressions*"—Examiner. "*It was in itself a thing so interesting as a development of English literature, that we are thankful to Mr. Friswell for reproducing, in a very elegant volume, the chief work of the gallant and chivalrous, the gay yet learned knight, who patronized the muse of Spenser, and fell upon the bloody field of Zutphen, leaving behind him a light of heroism and humane compassion which would shed an eternal glory on his name, though all he ever wrote had perished with himself.*"—London Review.

VII.

THE GENTLE LIFE. Second Series. Third Edition.

"*There is the same mingled power and simplicity which makes the author so emphatically a first-rate essayist, giving a fascination in each essay which will make this volume at least as popular as its elder brother.*"—Star. "*These essays are amongst the best in our language.*"—Public Opinion.

VIII.

VARIA: Readings from Rare Books. Reprinted, by permission, from the *Saturday Review, Spectator, &c.*

"*The books discussed in this volume are no less valuable than they are rare, but life is not long enough to allow a reader to wade through such thick folios, and therefore the compiler is entitled to the ratitude of the public for having sifted their contents, and thereby rendered their treasures available to the general reader.*"—Observer.

IX.

A CONCORDANCE OR VERBAL INDEX to the whole of Milton's Poetical Works. Comprising upwards of 20,000 References By Charles D. Cleveland, LL.D. With Vignette Portrait of Milton.

. This work affords an immediate reference to any passage in any edition of Milton's Poems, to which it may be justly termed an indispensable Appendix.

"*By the admirers of Milton the book will be highly appreciated, but its chief value will, if we mistake not, be found in the fact that it is a compact word-book of the English language.*"—Record. "*An invaluable Index, which the publishers have done a public service in reprinting.*"—Notes and Queries.

X.

THE SILENT HOUR: Essays, Original and Selected. By the Author of "The Gentle Life." Second Edition.

"*Out of twenty Essays five are from the Editor's pen, and he has selected the rest from the writings of Barrow, Baxter, Sherlock, Massillon, Latimer, Sandys, Jeremy Taylor, Huskin, and Izaac Walton. The selections have been made with taste and judgment, and the Editor's own contributions are not unworthy in themselves of a place in such distinguished company. The volume is avowedly meant 'for Sunday reading, and those who have not access to the originals of great authors may do worse on Sunday or any other afternoon, than fall back upon the 'Silent Hour' and the golden words of Jeremy Taylor and Massillon. All who possess the 'Gentle Life' should own this volume.*"—Standard.

XI.

ESSAYS ON ENGLISH WRITERS, for the Self-improvement of Students in English Literature.

"*The author has a distinct purpose and a proper and noble ambition to win the young to the pure and noble study of our glorious English literature. The book is too good intrinsically not to command a wide and increasing circulation, and its style is so pleasant and lively that it will find many readers among the educated classes, as well as among self-helpers. To all (both men and women) who have neglected to read and study their native literature we would certainly suggest the volume before us as a fitting introduction.*"—Examiner.

XII.

OTHER PEOPLE'S WINDOWS. By J. Hain Friswell. Second Edition.

"*The old project of a window in the bosom to render the soul of man visible, is what every honest fellow has a manifold reason to wish for.*"—Pope's Letters, Dec. 12, 1718.

"*The chapters are so lively in themselves, so mingled with shrewd views of human nature, so full of illustrative anecdotes, that the reader cannot fail to be amused. Written with remarkable power and effect. 'Other People's Windows' is distinguished by original and keen observation of life, as well as by lively and versatile power of narration.*"—Morning Post. "*We have not read a cleverer or more entertaining book for a long time.*" Observer. "*Some of the little stories are very graceful and tender, but Mr. Friswell's style is always bright and pleasant, and 'Other People's Windows' is just the book to lie upon the drawing-room table, and be read by snatches at idle moments.*"—Guardian.

LITERATURE, WORKS OF REFERENCE, ETC.

HE Origin and History of the English Language, and of the early literature it embodies. By the Hon. George P. Marsh, U. S. Minister at Turin, Author of "Lectures on the English Language." 8vo. cloth extra, 16s.

Lectures on the English Language; forming the Introductory Series to the foregoing Work. By the same Author. 8vo. Cloth, 16s. This is the only author's edition.

Man and Nature; or, Physical Geography as Modified by Human Action. By George P. Marsh, Author of "Lectures on the English Language," &c. 8vo. cloth, 14s.

> "*Mr. Marsh, well known as the author of two of the most scholarly works yet published on the English language, sets himself in excellent spirit, and with immense learning, to indicate the character, and, approximately, the extent of the changes produced by human action in the physical condition of the globe we inhabit. The whole of Mr. Marsh's book is an eloquent showing of the duty of care in the establishment of harmony between man's life and the forces of nature, so as to bring to their highest points the fertility of the soil, the vigour of the animal life, and the salubrity of the climate, on which we have to depend for the physical well-being of mankind.*"—Examiner.

Her Majesty's Mails: a History of the Post Office, and an Industrial Account of its Present Condition. By Wm. Lewins, of the General Post Office. 2nd Edition, revised and enlarged, with a Photographic Portrait of Sir Rowland Hill. Small post 8vo. 6s.

A History of Banks for Savings; including a full account of the origin and progress of Mr. Gladstone's recent prudential measures. By William Lewins, Author of "Her Majesty's Mails." 8vo. cloth, 12s.

The English Catalogue of Books: giving the date of publication of every book published from 1835 to 1863, in addition to the title, size, price, and publisher, in one alphabet. An entirely new work, combining the Copyrights of the "London Catalogue" and the "British Catalogue." One thick volume of 900 pages, half morocco, 45s.

> *,* The Annual Catalogue of Books published during 1863 with Index of Subjects. 8vo. 5s.

Index to the Subjects of Books published in the United Kingdom during the last Twenty Years—1837-1857. Containing as many as 74,000 references, under subjects, so as to ensure immediate reference to the books on the subject required, each giving title, price, publisher, and date. Two valuable Appendices are also given—A, containing full lists of all Libraries, Collections, Series, and Miscellanies—and B, a List of Literary Societies, Printing Societies, and their Issues. One vol. royal 8vo. Morocco, 1l. 6s.

> *,* Volume II. from 1857 in Preparation.

Outlines of Moral Philosophy. By Dugald Stewart, Professor of Moral Philosophy in the University of Edinburgh, with Memoir, &c. By James McCosh, LL.D. New Edition, 12mo. 3s. 6d.

A Dictionary of Photography, on the Basis of Sutton's Dictionary.
Rewritten by Professor Dawson, of King's College, Editor of the "Journal
of Photography;" and Thomas Sutton, B.A., Editor of "Photograph
Notes." 8vo. with numerous Illustrations. 8s. 6d.

Dr. Worcester's New and Greatly Enlarged Dictionary of the
English Language. Adapted for Library or College Reference, comprising 40,000 Words more than Johnson's Dictionary. 4to. cloth, 1,834 pp.
price 31s. 6d. well bound.

" The volumes before us show a vast amount of diligence; but with
Webster it is diligence in combination with fancifulness,—with Worcester in combination with good sense and judgment. Worcester's is the
soberer and safer book, and may be pronounced the best existing English
Lexicon."—*Athenæum.*

The Publishers' Circular, and General Record of British and
Foreign Literature; giving a transcript of the title-page of every work
published in Great Britain, and every work of interest published abroad,
with lists of all the publishing houses.
    Published regularly on the 1st and 15th of every Month, and forwarded
post free to all parts of the world on payment of 8s. per annum.

A Handbook to the Charities of London.   By Sampson Low,
Jun. Comprising an Account of upwards of 800 Institutions chiefly in
London and its Vicinity. A Guide to the Benevolent and to the Unfor-
tunate. Cloth limp, 1s. 6d.

Prince Albert's Golden Precepts.   *Second Edition,* with Photograph. A Memorial of the Prince Consort; comprising Maxims and
Extracts from Addresses of His late Royal Highness. Many now for
the first time collected and carefully arranged. With an Index. Royal
16mo. beautifully printed on toned paper, cloth, gilt edges, 2s. 6d.

Our Little Ones in Heaven; Thoughts in Prose and Verse, selected from the Writings of favourite Authors; with Frontispiece after
Sir Joshua Reynolds. Fcap. 8vo. cloth extra. Second Edition. 3s. 6d.

BIOGRAPHY, TRAVEL, AND ADVENTURE.

HE Life of John James Audubon, the Naturalist, including his Romantic Adventures in the back woods of
America. Correspondence with celebrated Europeans, &c.
Edited, from materials supplied by his widow, by Robert Buchanan. 8vo. With portraits, price 15s.

" *A readable book, with many interesting and some thrilling pages in
it.*"—*Athenæum.* " *From first to last, the biography teems with interesting
adventures, with amusing or perilous incidents, with curious gossip, with
picturesque description.*"—*Daily News.* " *But, as we have said, Audubon
could write as well as draw; and while his portfolio was a cause of wonder
to even such men as Cuvier, Wilson, and Sir Thomas Lawrence, his diary
contained a number of spirited sketches of the places he had visited, which
cannot fail to interest and even to delight the reader.*"—*Examiner.*

Leopold the First, King of the Belgians; from unpublished documents, by Theodore Juste. Translated by Robert Black, M.A.

" *A readable biography of the wise and good King Leopold is certain to be read in England.*"—Daily News. " *A more important contribution to historical literature has not for a long while been furnished.*"—Bell's Messenger. " *Of great value to the future historian, and will interest politicians even now.*"—Spectator. " *The subject is of interest, and the story is narrated without excess of enthusiasm or depreciation. The translation by Mr. Black is executed with correctness, yet not without a graceful ease. This end is not often attained in translations so nearly verbal as this ; the book itself deserves to become popular in England.*"—Athenæum.

Fredrika Bremer's Life, Letters, and Posthumous Works. Edited by her sister, Charlotte Bremer; translated from the Swedish by Fred. Milow. Post 8vo. cloth. 10s. 6d.

The Rise and Fall of the Emperor Maximilian: an Authentic History of the Mexican Empire, 1861-7. Together with the Imperial Correspondence. With Portrait, 8vo. price 10s. 6d.

Madame Recamier, Memoirs and Correspondence of. Translated from the French and edited by J. M. Luyster. With Portrait. Crown 8vo. 7s. 6d.

Plutarch's Lives. An entirely new Library Edition, carefully revised and corrected, with some Original Translations by the Editor. Edited by A. H. Clough, Esq. sometime Fellow of Oriel College, Oxford, and late Professor of English Language and Literature at University College. 5 vols. 8vo. cloth. 2l. 10s.

Social Life of the Chinese: a Daguerreotype of Daily Life in China. Condensed from the Work of the Rev. J. Doolittle, by the Rev. Paxton Hood. With above 100 Illustrations. Post 8vo. price 8s. 6d.

The Open Polar Sea: a Narrative of a Voyage of Discovery towards the North Pole. By Dr. Isaac I. Hayes. An entirely new and cheaper edition. With Illustrations. Small post 8vo. 6s.

The Physical Geography of the Sea and its Meteorology ; or, the Economy of the Sea and its Adaptations, its Salts, its Waters, its Climates, its Inhabitants, and whatever there may be of general interest in its Commercial Uses or Industrial Pursuits. By Commander M. F. Maury, LL.D New Edition. With Charts. Post 8vo. cloth extra.

Captain Hall's Life with the Esquimaux. New and cheaper Edition, with Coloured Engravings and upwards of 100 Woodcuts. With a Map. Price 7s. 6d. cloth extra; Forming the cheapest and most popular Edition of a work on Arctic Life and Exploration ever published.

Christian Heroes in the Army and Navy. By Charles Rogers, LL.D. Author of " Lyra Britannica." Crown 8vo. 3s. 6d.

The Black Country and its Green Border Land ; or, Expeditions and Explorations round Birmingham, Wolverhampton, &c. By Elihu Burritt. Second and cheaper edition, post 8vo. 6s.

A Walk from London to John O'Groats, and from London to the Land's End and Back. With Notes by the Way. By Elihu Burritt Two vols. price 6s. each, with Illustrations.

The Voyage Alone; a Sail in the " Yawl, Rob Roy." By John
M'Gregor. With Illustrations. Price 5s.

*Also, uniform, by the same Author, with Maps and numerous Illus-
trations, price 5s. each.*

A Thousand Miles in the Rob Roy Canoe, on Rivers and Lakes of
Europe. Fifth edition.

The Rob Roy on the Baltic. A Canoe Voyage in Norway, Sweden, &c.

NEW BOOKS FOR YOUNG PEOPLE.

 ILD Life under the Equator. By Paul Du Chaillu,
Author of " Discoveries in Equatorial Africa." With 40
Original Illustrations, price 6s.

> " *M. du Chaillu's name will be a sufficient guarantee for the interest of
> Wild Life under the Equator, which he has narrated for young people in
> a very readable volume.*"—Times. " *M. Du Chaillu proves a good writer
> for the young, and he has skilfully utilized his experience for their benefit.*"
> —Economist. " *The author possesses an immense advantage over other
> writers of Adventures for boys, and this is secure for a popular run: it
> is at once light, racy, and attractive.*"—Illustrated Times.

Also by the same Author, uniform.

Stories of the Gorilla Country, 36 Illustrations.   Price 6s.

> " *It would be hard to find a more interesting book for boys than this.*"—
> Times. " *Young people will obtain from it a very considerable amount
> of information touching the manners and customs, ways and means of
> Africans, and of course great amusement in the accounts of the Gorilla.
> The book is really a meritorious work, and is elegantly got up.*"—Athenæum.

Cast Away in the Cold. An Old Man's Story of a Young Man's
Adventures. By the Author of " The Open Polar Sea." With Illustrations. Small 8vo. cloth extra, price 6s.

> " *The result is delightful. A story of adventure of the most telling
> local colour and detail, the most exciting danger, and ending with the most
> natural and effective escape. There is an air of veracity and reality
> about the tale which Capt. Hayes could scarcely help giving to an Arctic
> adventure of any kind. There is great vivacity and picturesqueness in
> the style, the illustrations are admirable, and there is a novelty in the
> 'dénouement' which greatly enhances the pleasure with which we lay the
> book down. This story of the two Arctic Crusoes will long remain one of
> the most powerful of children's stories, as it assuredly deserves to be one
> of the most popular.*"—Spectator.

The Silver Skates; a Story of Holland Life. By Mrs. M. A.
Dodge. Edited by W. H. G. Kingston. Illustrated, cloth extra, 3s. 6d.

The Voyage of the Constance; a tale of the Polar Seas. By
Mary Gillies. With 8 Illustrations by Charles Keene. Fcap. 3s. 6d.

Life amongst the North and South American Indians. By George Catlin. And Last Rambles amongst the Indians beyond the Rocky Mountains and the Andes. With numerous Illustrations by the Author. 2 vols. small post 8vo. 5s. each, cloth extra.

"*An admirable book, full of useful information, wrapt up in stories peculiarly adapted to rouse the imagination and stimulate the curiosity of boys and girls. To compare a book with 'Robinson Crusoe,' and to say that it sustains such comparison, is to give it high praise indeed.*"—Athenæum.

Our Salt and Fresh Water Tutors; a Story of that Good Old Time—Our School Days at the Cape. Edited by W. H. G. Kingston. With Illustrations, price 3s. 6d.

"*One of the best books of the kind that the season has given us. This little book is to be commended warmly.*"—Illustrated Times.

The Boy's Own Book of Boats. A Description of every Craft that sails upon the waters; and how to Make, Rig, and Sail Model Boats, by W. H. G. Kingston, with numerous Illustrations by E. Weedon. Second edition, enlarged. Fcap. 8vo. 3s. 6d.

" *This well-written, well-wrought book.*"—Athenæum.

Also by the same Author,

Ernest Bracebridge; or, Boy's Own Book of Sports. 3s. 6d.
The Fire Ships. A Story of the Days of Lord Cochrane. 5s.
The Cruise of the Frolic. 5s.
Jack Buntline: the Life of a Sailor Boy. 2s.

The Autobiography of a Small Boy. By the Author of " School Days at Saxonhurst." Fcap. 8vo. cloth, 5s. [*Nearly ready.*

Also now ready.

Alwyn Morton, his School and his Schoolfellows. 5s.
Stanton Grange; or, Life at a Tutor's. By the Rev. C. J. Atkinson. 5s.

Phenomena and Laws of Heat : a Volume of Marvels of Science. By Achille Cazin. Translated and Edited by Elihu Rich. With numerous Illustrations. Fcap. 8vo. price 5s.

Also, uniform, same price.

Marvels of Optics. By F. Marion. Edited and Translated by C. W. Quin. With 70 Illustrations. 5s.

Marvels of Thunder and Lightning. By De Fonvielle. Edited by Dr. Phipson. Full of Illustrations. 5s.

Stories of the Great Prairie. From the Novels of J. F. Cooper. Illustrated. Price 5s.

Also, uniform, same price.

Stories of the Woods, from the Adventures of Leather-Stocking.
Stories of the Sea, from Cooper's Naval Novels.
The Voyage of the Constance. By Mary Gillies. 3s. 6d.
The Swiss Family Robinson, and Sequel. In 1 vol. 3s. 6d.
The Story Without an End. Translated by Sarah Austin. 2s. 6d.

Under the Waves; or the Hermit Crab in Society. By Annie
E. Ridley. Impl. 16mo. cloth extra, with coloured illustration   Cloth,
4s.; gilt edges, 4s. 6d.

Also beautifully Illustrated:—

Little Bird Red and Little Bird Blue. Coloured. 5s.
Snow-Flakes, and what they told the Children. Coloured, 5s.
Child's Book of the Sagacity of Animals. 5s.; or coloured, 7s. 6d.
Child's Picture Fable Book. 5s.; or coloured, 7s. 6d.
Child's Treasury of Story Books. 5s.; or coloured, 7s. 6d.
The Nursery Playmate. 200 Pictures. 5s.; or coloured, 9s.

Adventures on the Great Hunting-Grounds of the World. From
the Frence of Victor Meunier. With additional matter, including the
Duke of Edinburgh's Elephant Hunt, &c. With 22 Engravings,
price 5s.

"*The book for all boys in whom the love of travel and adventure is
strong. They will find here plenty to amuse them and much to instruct
them besides.*"—Times.

Also, lately published.

One Thousand Miles in the Rob Roy Canoe. By John Macgregor, M.A. 5s.
The Rob Roy on the Baltic. By the same Author. 5s.
Sailing Alone; or, 1,500 Miles Voyage in the Yawl Rob Roy. By the
same Author. 5s.
Golden Hair; a Tale of the Pilgrim Fathers. By Sir Lascelles Wraxall. 5s.
Black Panther : a Boy's Adventures amongst the Red Skins. By the
same Author. 5s.

Anecdotes of the Queen and Royal Family of England. Collected,
arranged, and edited, for the more especial use of Colonial Readers, by
J. George Hodgins, LL.D., F.R.G.S., Deputy-Superintendent of Educa-
tion for the Province of Ontario. With Illustrations. Price 5s.

Geography for my Children. By Mrs. Harriet Beecher Stowe.
Author of "Uncle Tom's Cabin," &c. Arranged and Edited by an Eng-
lish Lady, under the Direction of the Authoress. With upwards of Fifty
Illustrations. Cloth extra, 4s. 6d.

Child's Play. Illustrated with Sixteen Coloured Drawings by
E. V. B., printed in fac-simile by W. Dickes' process, and ornamented
with Initial Letters. New edition, with India paper tints, royal 8vo.
cloth extra, bevelled cloth, 7s. 6d. The Original Edition of this work
was published at One Guinea.

Little Gerty; or, the First Prayer, selected and abridged from
"The Lamplighter." By a Lady. Price 6d. Particularly adapted
for a Sunday School Gift Book.

Great Fun and More Fun for our Little Friends. By Harriet
Myrtle. With Edward Wehnert's Pictures. 2 vols. each 5s.

BELLES LETTRES, FICTION, &c.

THE LOG OF MY LEISURE HOURS: a Story of
Real Life. By an Old Sailor. 3 vols. post 8vo. 24s.
"*If people do not read ' The Log' it will have failed as
regards them ; but it is a success in every sense of the word as
regards its author. It deserves to succeed.*"—Morning Post.

David Gray ; and other Essays, chiefly on Poetry. By Robert
Buchanan. In one vol. fcap. 8vo. price 6s.

The Book of the Sonnet; being Selections, with an Essay on
Sonnets and Sonneteers. By the late Leigh Hunt. Edited, from the
original MS. with Additions, by S. Adams Lee. 2 vols. price 18s.
"*Reading a book of this sort should make us feel proud of our language
and of our literature, and proud also of that cultivated common nature
which can raise so many noble thoughts and images out of this hard, sullen
world into a thousand enduring forms of beauty. The ' Book of the Sonnet' should be a classic, and the professor as well as the student of English
will find it a work of deep interest and completeness.*"—London Review.

Lyra Sacra Americana: Gems of American Poetry, selected
with Notes and Biographical Sketches by C. D. Cleveland, D.D., Author
of the " Milton Concordance." 18mo., cloth, gilt edges. Price 4s. 6d.

Poems of the Inner Life. Selected chiefly from modern Authors,
by permission. Small post 8vo. 6s.; gilt edges, 6s. 6d.

English and Scotch Ballads, &c. An extensive Collection.
With Notices of the kindred Ballads of other Nations. Edited by F. J.
Child. 8 vols. fcap. cloth, 3s. 6d. each.

The Autocrat of the Breakfast Table. By Oliver Wendell
Holmes, LL.D. Popular Edition, 1s. Illustrated Edition, choicely
printed, cloth extra, 6s.

The Professor at the Breakfast Table. By Oliver Wendell Holmes,
Author of "The Autocrat of the Breakfast-Table." Cheap Edition,
fcap. 3s. 6d.

Bee-keeping. By "The Times" Bee-master. Small post 8vo.
numerous illustrations, cloth, 5s.
"*Our friend the Bee-master has the knack of exposition, and knows how
to tell a story well ; over and above which, he tells a story so that thousands
can take a practical, and not merely a speculative interest in it.*"—Times.

Queer Little People. By the Author of " Uncle Tom's Cabin."
Fcap. 1s. Also by the same Author.
The Little Foxes that Spoil the Grapes, 1s.
House and Home Papers, 1s.
The Pearl of Orr's Island, Illustrated by Gilbert, 5s.
The Minister's Wooing. Illustrated by Phiz, 5s.

The Story of Four Little Women: Meg, Joe, Beth, and Amy.
By Louisa M. Alcott. With Illustrations. 16mo, cloth 3s. 6d.
"*A bright, cheerful, healthy story—with a tinge of thoughtful gravity
about it which reminds one of John Bunyan. Meg going to Vanity Fair
is a chapter written with great cleverness and a pleasant humour.*"—
Guardian.

Also, Entertaining Stories for Young Ladies. 3s. 6d. each, cloth, gilt edges.

Helen Felton's Question: a Book for Girls. By Agnes Wylde.
Faith Gartney's Girlhood. By Mrs. D. T. Whitney. Seventh thousand.
The Gayworthys. By the same Author. Third Edition.
A Summer in Leslie Goldthwaite's Life. By the same Author.
The Masque at Ludlow. By the Author of " Mary Powell."
Miss Biddy Frobisher: a Salt Water Story. By the same Author.
Selvaggio; a Story of Italy. By the same Author. New Edition.
The Journal of a Waiting Gentlewoman. By a new Author. New Edition
The Shady Side and the Sunny Side. Two Tales of New England.

Marian; or, the Light of Some One's Home.   By Maud Jeanne
Franc. Small post 8vo., 5s.

Also, by the same Author.

Emily's Choice: an Australian Tale. 5s.
Vermont Vale: or, Home Pictures in Australia. 5s.

Tauchnitz's English Editions of German Authors. Each volume
cloth flexible, 2s.; or sewed, 1s. 6d. The following are now ready :—

1. On the Heights. By B. Auerbach. 3 vols.
2. In the Year '13. By Fritz Reuter. 1 vol.
3. Faust. By Goethe. 1 vol.
4. Undine, and other Tales. By Fouqué. 1 vol.
5. L'Arrabiata. By Paul Heyse. 1 vol.
6. The Princess, and other Tales. By Heinrich Zschokke. 1 vol.
7. Lessing's Nathan the Wise.
8. Hacklander's Behind the Counter, translated by Mary Howitt.

Low's Copyright Cheap Editions of American Authors.   A
thoroughly good and cheap series of editions, which, whilst combining
every advantage that can be secured by the best workmanship at the
lowest possible rate, will possess an additional claim on the reading
public by providing for the remuneration of the American author and
the legal protection of the English publisher. Ready :—

1. Haunted Hearts. By the Author of " The Lamplighter."
2. The Guardian Angel. By " The Autocrat of the Breakfast Table."
3. The Minister's Wooing. By the Author of " Uncle Tom's Cabin."

To be followed by a New Volume on the first of every alternate month.
Each complete in itself, printed from new type, with Initial Letters and Orna-
ments, and published at the low price of 1s. 6d. stiff cover, or 2s. cloth.

LONDON: SAMPSON LOW, SON, AND MARSTON,
CROWN BUILDINGS, 188, FLEET STREET.
English, American, and Colonial Booksellers and Publishers.

Chiswick Press:—Whittingham and Wilkins, Tooks Court, Chancery Lane

.